ESCAPING INFINTY

Richard Paolinelli

TUSCANY
BAY
PUBLISHING

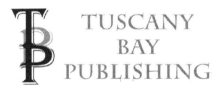

Other Tuscany Bay Publishing titles
by Richard Paolinelli

Maelstrom
The Invited (Novelette)
Legacy of Death (Novelette)
From The Fields (Non-Fiction)
Perfection's Arbiter (Non-Fiction)

Argus Book titles by Richard Paolinelli

Reservations
Betrayals

Belanger Books Sherlock Holmes anthologies with stories by Richard Paolinelli

Beyond Watson (A Lesson In Mercy)
Holmes Away From Home (The Woman Returns)

Website: www.richardpaolinelli.com

Facebook: Author Richard Paolinelli
(www.facebook.com/profile.php?id=100013966861775)
Twitter: @ScribesShade

Front Book Cover Design by RockingBookCovers.com

ESCAPING INFINITY

ISBN: 978-1541392588

This novel is a work of fiction, and any similarity
to any real persons or situations is purely coincidental.

To my former teacher, Charles V. Wells,

for instilling a love of the science

behind all of my beloved science fiction.

PROLOGUE

Molten lava—an angry mixture of searing hot glowing reds, oranges and yellows—flowed out from large cracks in the blackened rock, but no sooner had the lava fought its way to the surface, it almost instantly cooled and hardened to solid rock in the piercing cold of deep space that enveloped the sphere. This barren planet, which orbited a mere ninety million miles from its parent star, had no atmosphere with which it could trap the warmth from its core and the sun. Nor was there an atmosphere to protect the surface from the harsh, unforgiving vacuum.

At least, the small rocky world didn't have an atmosphere any longer.

For it had in fact once been a thriving, living world of seas, deserts, forests and plains. It had also been filled with a nearly uncountable variety of life surviving in climates that ran from the one extreme of frigid cold to the other of blistering heat. That there were so many more climates that lay between the extremes had made the little world almost unique in the universe. The billions of life forms that had, until very recently, called this planet home had ranged from the microscopic and on up to a dominant species on the cusp of incredible greatness. This species had been ready to take their final step into deep space travel and thus join all of the other space-faring civilizations that had long waited to greet them from every corner of the galaxy.

Millions of years of evolution and progress had brought them to this day and all of it had been consumed in an inferno of such magnitude that they could never have imagined. All of it gone, vaporized in less than a minute, as time had been measured on their world.

There was nothing left now but this dismal, lifeless ball of rock that bled lava from the cracks in its core. Every volcano, some dormant for millennia, that had dotted the surface, above and below where the seas and oceans had once resided, now became hyperactive. What little water that was left on the planet's surface, which had once been nearly seventy percent submerged under the water and ice—had collected into poisonous, radioactive pools in the deepest craters and had frozen solid even faster than the lava had. If that water were ever to return to its unfrozen state, it would likely just barely cover one or two percent of the surface now and no living thing would survive in it, or after consuming it, for very long.

The planet's death throes had reached out for hundreds of thousands of miles to leave its mark on the planet's lone companion moon. Already heavily cratered by past eons of meteor impacts, the moon now displayed several wide fracture lines that ran in great zigzag patterns across its face. The moon itself was still ringing, the dust on its surface vibrating as if being sifted through a giant invisible screen, from the impact of the shockwave generated by its companion's demise. The wave had struck the moon full on and had redirected every celestial body that orbited near the dead planet in a two-million-mile radius.

The ringing would eventually subside. The moon would hold together and not shatter to become a set of rings around the planet, but it would forever bear those terrible marks left behind by its companion's demise.

The moon's orbital path had been increased by the shockwave as well. It would now take it three more of the dead planet's days for it to complete the single circuit around the planet than it had before the destruction occurred.

Lying just beyond that new orbital path was a fleet of eight spaceships, shaped like sleek, black boomerangs. Graceful and looking like pieces of art despite their massive size, the ships sat unmoving in space, silently watching the grim scene as it unfolded before them. Seven of these ships were clustered together in formation. The eighth, which served as the fleet's flagship, had taken up station a few thousand miles closer to the dead planet and its scarred moon.

The bridge of that flagship was perched atop the command pod that rested just at the point where the two wings joined. At the end of each wing tip perched the engines which powered the ship through space at faster than light speeds that violated every law of physics the former inhabitants of the now dead planet had ever known.

The bridge of the flagship, like those on the other seven ships of the fleet, was also as quiet as the grave.

How fitting, the fleet's commander thought to himself as he stared at the horror being displayed on the bridge's main view screen, *for this is truly a grave we are visiting and the corpse's very murderers are its only mourners attending its funeral service.*

The fleet commander, an old veteran of his world's centuries-old space exploration, had visited this very planet many times during his travels before. He had never once failed to find something new to marvel at, especially when it came to the life forms that had called this place home. He had never before seen its equal anywhere else in the universe. Even as much as he loved his home world, it was a pale, ugly husk when compared to this bright jewel. It was all gone now, snuffed out in a searing flash of heat and fire the planet had never before seen. It was all destroyed, completely and utterly, and in the cruelest of ironies it was all due to his vanity, by his very own order.

A gasping, choking sound interrupted the silence. It was the sound one made when trying to breathe in past the tears and found the way blocked beyond all bearing. It was desperately trying not to become a sob, lest it then became a wail and then a never-ending scream. The fleet commander tore his gaze away from the horror on the view screen, looking down and to his left at the source of the wretched sound.

The source was his navigator, a young man barely older than the fleet commander's own youngest child, and his tears were still streaming down his face as he gazed at the nightmarish scene on the screen above his station. There on the console were the same young hands that had set the course and had brought the fleet here to an awful destiny. The fleet commander gently laid his hand on the child's shoulder—he had always thought of every member of his many crews as his children and today more so than ever before—and he felt the initial flinch and the trembling underneath his hand.

"This was not your fault," the fleet commander said in a soft, soothing tone. "The order to divert here was mine, as is all of the blame for this terrible tragedy. Do not let it weigh on you."

It was true, although he could not blame the child for not believing a single word of it, any more than he would have if their positions had been reversed. The fleet commander had ordered the course change and the navigator had dutifully entered it. But instead of exiting from hyperspace at a safe distance from the planet, all eight ships and exited directly within the atmosphere of the planet below. They had quickly passed through and back into space, a transit of only a handful of seconds, but the energy released by their sudden appearance in the sky had ignited the planet's atmosphere. In very little time, everything had been scoured away from the surface, every drop of water from the oceans had been boiled away and the upper layers of the atmosphere blasted into space, forming the shockwave that had so dramatically impacted its moon. The wave of heat and radiation had swiftly reached out and destroyed all of the artificial satellites that orbited the planet, instantly killing all of the creatures that inhabited a small handful of them.

"It wasn't your fault," the fleet commander repeated softly.

That much was true, in a sense at least. The course the navigator had input had been perfectly correct. But the navigation computer had failed to flag a very small star near their new course. This star was unexpectedly collapsing into a black hole. The change in gravitational pull was very slight at this early stage of the star's transition, but it was just enough of an increase to impact the fleet's passage through that area of space. The alteration had changed their exit point within the solar system by a microscopic percentage of a degree, but it had a very dramatic effect.

Instead of exiting from hyperspace well behind the moon, where they could observe the planet safe from any possible detection from the planet or any of its satellites, all eight ships had exited some twelve miles above the surface of the planet. In mere seconds, they had passed through the atmosphere and slipped back into space but the damage had already been done. The fleet commander supposed it could be considered no small miracle that the same forces that had ignited the atmosphere, boiled the oceans into vapor and cracked the planet's core in several places hadn't ripped all of his ships to pieces as well. Perhaps it would have been more just if his fleet had perished along with the doomed planet.

They had discovered the error only after the tragedy had unfolded, when nothing could be done to prevent it. Discovering the reason why the computer had failed would take a great deal of time and investigation.

Little good that knowledge will do for the dead below, the fleet commander thought bitterly as he returned his gaze to the screen. The planet's lone natural satellite began to rise into view from behind the planet. He had witnessed this event many times in his past visits, the moon slipping above the horizon and passing through the atmosphere as if swimming through water before exiting out to shine brightly and clearly on the surface below.

Now, with no atmospheric distortion to transit through, the sight of the visibly scarred moon rising from behind the abomination that had been a vibrant world now struck the fleet commander as utterly obscene.

An entire, honorable career of exploration and discovery, all that I have accomplished and learned through the long years, he thought as he kept his eyes on the screen in a sort of self-imposed punishment, *and this is what will serve as my final legacy. Planet-killer.*

His second-in-command, who had served with him for ten cycles now and was long overdue for his own command, quietly entered the bridge and approached his commander. His eyes, as was the case with anyone who stepped onto any of the eight bridges in the fleet, could not help but immediately look toward the screen. With an effort, he pulled them away from the terrible scene and softly spoke to the fleet commander.

"They have all arrived on board," he reported softly. "They are all waiting for you below, sir."

"They" would be the commanding officers of the other seven ships in the fleet of course. They had all transported over to the flagship to meet with their fleet's commander in light of the tragedy, to discuss what they should do. Stay here, continue on with the original mission or return home and report their role in the disaster. The fleet commander nodded wordlessly in reply as he turned away from the screen and caught the downward glance from his second that was directed at the shaken navigator. It was a questioning look, asking if the boy should be relieved of his post.

No, the fleet commander's quick shake of the head answered. *Pull him off the bridge now and you send the message that we are blaming him for this tragedy. Leave him at his station and let him know his crew and his commanding officers stand with him.*

The entire exchange was swift and silent; the two had served together for far too long to need words now. They both knew the pain the other was feeling and both knew they would set aside the pain and the grief for later and do their duty now.

The fleet commander strode for the bridge's main exit to meet with his colleagues and try to decide what they should do next. He already knew they could not undo the carnage. While temporal travel was a proven possibility, it was also proven that an attempt to undo an event of this magnitude would result in even more damage to the fabric of time and space. Not only would the inhabitants of this planet still likely die, but many other planets would likely suffer the same fate.

They would try to find a way of course, but the sad truth might be they would not be able to find any possible way at all to make this right.

"Sir," his communications officer called out before he could depart from the bridge. "Should we send a report back home to the Council?"

"Not yet." He replied after a moment's pause. "Let us wait awhile longer until we decide if there is anything we can do here first. Then I will send them a full report."

"Yes, sir," she acknowledged. "Sir, I…"

Her voice drifted off as she was unable to find the words to express her feelings. Her commanding officer understood that all too well.

"I know," he said softly. "Carry on."

"Yes, sir."

With a final glance back at his bridge, seeing his second quietly speaking with the stricken navigator to offer whatever comfort that he could, the fleet commander stepped off bridge and entered the transport tube to take him to his meeting with the other commanders. They could discuss the matter to infinity for all the good it would do them, but in his heart he knew they would never be able to find a way to make it right.

What had begun as a grand final mission for one of their civilization's greatest explorers, a first-ever voyage to the very center of the known universe, had ended almost as soon as it had begun. This innocent detour had been intended to show those under his command why they were out here. They sought out new life and stood ready to welcome it into the galactic family when the time was right.

This planet had been his career's greatest achievement, even though he'd likely never live long enough to see his world make official contact with it. He had discovered it during one of his first expeditions and in an area of the galaxy that many had written off as completely barren of intelligent life. They were forbidden from contacting the planet's inhabitants until they had reached a certain level of technological advance and, despite the species just beginning landings on its moon and sending out probes to its system's planets, this planet wasn't quite there yet.

So they observed unnoticed, which became increasingly harder to do with each passing visit. As it was, the fleet commander wasn't convinced they hadn't been spotted that first time by the crew of the craft landing on the moon. But they continued to observe as the young species struggled through the growing pains every civilization faced. Most made it, some sadly did not. So the explorers settled in to watch from afar, hoping for and eagerly awaiting the day when they could step out of hiding and officially welcome their new brothers and sisters.

And now that day would never come.

Then, and only then, in the privacy of the tube and away from the sight of his crew, did he finally allow his head to bow, his shoulders to sag and openly weep for all that they had destroyed.

ONE

I think I am a pretty honest enough guy to admit this: I really have no one but myself to blame for the mess that I found myself in. After all, I'd been doing this long enough. Or, as they say here in the American Southwest, this wasn't my first rodeo. So I really should have known there would be no other possible outcome other than the one I was currently experiencing.

We were lost.

And by lost I don't mean the "oh hell, we're on the wrong side of town" kind of lost either. I mean the "we are likely not going to see another living being for a very long time and when we finally do find one, they might not speak the same language as we do" kind of good and lost.

No matter which way you chose to look in, it was the same in every direction. Nothing but flat, barren land of sand and clumps of dry yellowing scrub grass as far as the eye could see. There was an occasional shrub of pale green here or there and maybe a lizard or two skittering across the road in a feeble attempt to break the monotony. But there was absolutely no sign of civilization anywhere near where we were.

I couldn't suppress a sigh.

It was not the long-suffering type of sigh reserved for someone enduring the most bone-crushing despair. Or of one who had just lost the love of one's life. Or even of one who had endured much and simply couldn't endure any more. No, this was the sigh one makes when no other sound or expression could possibly convey the depth of desolate despair that came with the realization that all hope was indeed lost.

Or someone helplessly—even hopelessly—stuck in a car on a long road trip shortly after Charlie Womack had decided to take one of his infamous "shortcuts."

Now please, don't get me wrong. I love the guy like a brother. You simply could not ask for a better wingman on a Friday night. There was just something about the guy—despite him being just this side of chubby with unruly black hair that seemed to try to go off in every direction simultaneously above the always goofy expression on his face—that seemed to bring out the "mothering" instincts in all of the ladies over at Cassity's Pub back in Denver.

The benefit of his presence, of course, of having a flock of single young women hovering around Charlie for me was that I tended to draw the attention of those women who were looking for something more than just "mothering" a man. It probably didn't hurt my chances too much that even when Charlie made the effort to look neat, he always appeared just a little too unkempt, for lack of a better term.

I had a height advantage on him of at least five inches and it had been so long since I had been any heavier than one eighty that I swore my bathroom scale just lit up "180" without even waiting for me to step on it. While I didn't go too overboard on keeping up appearances, I did keep the hair cut pretty short and the clothing as conservative and neat as possible.

I'd heard that the staff back at our office started a contest some time ago. The first one to spot a hair out of place, or even so much as a speck of lint on my jacket, won the pool. At last report, they were still waiting for a winner.

But I digress. Suffice it to say that neither one of us lacked for the companionship of the opposite sex, even though neither of us was really looking for anything long term for that matter. It had been that way the last fifteen years or so, since we first met each other back in college. Seeing as how it worked for us, we didn't change it.

This mutually beneficial partnership worked in our professional life as well. No sooner had the two of us walked off the campus with our respective Master's degrees in Mechanical Engineering—Charlie had a Bachelor's in Civil Engineering while I had a Bachelor's in Architectural Engineering—than we found ourselves heavily recruited by the firm of Pinelli, Gonzales and Hall.

I'm sure you've heard of them. They were only the top architectural firm in the country when it came to major metropolitan projects, like that recent remodel of the Twin Cities International Airport for example. Yes, in case you were wondering, Charlie and I were a big part of that job. And that was just one of many projects we had worked on around the world.

Let me tell you, when Old Man Pinelli himself—the guy who merely founded the entire company back in the day—showed up in person at our graduation to recruit us, it was a pretty big boost to the old ego. Needless to say, he didn't have to ask twice and Charlie and I quickly packed our belongings and headed off for the company's headquarters in Denver.

It hadn't taken long for Charlie Womack and Peter Childress—that's me by the way—to start getting noticed by everyone in the industry. A neat little mass transit remodel in the small but growing community of Turlock, California earned us a nice spread as the latest wunderkinds in *The Engineering Journal* early in our careers. Since then, it had been nothing but one success after another, along with some very impressive bonuses and pay raises I might add.

And while most of the other engineers in the company got paired up with new faces on a regular basis, the Old Man decreed that Charlie and I were a permanent team as long as we were at PGH. Like I said earlier, it worked and we had no complaints and neither did the Old Man.

Well, perhaps with the lone exception of being in my case when Charlie dragged us off on one of his thrice-accursed shortcuts that is.

This one had come because Charlie had discovered some hole-in-the-wall café just a little south of Gallup, New Mexico that served up its world-famous 'Cowboy Cobbler" and Charlie just had to try it. I had visions of a stringy, tough-to-chew glop when we first pulled up to the place. They were taking the Old West theme seriously and the place was filled with the aroma of seared animal flesh from the open grill. I got to watch my food get cooked here. As long as I wasn't looking for meat and bread, I would be okay. Vegetables were in short supply. When it came time for the "must have" dessert, it turned out to be a peach cobbler, served in enormous portions with at least a gallon of vanilla ice cream piled on top.

Ok, I'll admit it. It was pretty damn good. All of it, even the Cowboy Cobbler. But it certainly was not good enough to warrant getting lost over.

"Are you sure we're even on the right road anymore?" I shouted over the billowing wind at Charlie, who was seated behind the wheel of his prized fire engine red 1957 Pontiac Star Chief convertible. Oddly enough, it was the only thing of his that was kept in pristine condition and stayed that way all of the time. I had to shout the question at him because going fifty miles an hour with the top down created a lot of very noisy wind that hard to hear over.

I shot a quick glance over at the fuel gauge which showed below the quarter mark. That meant roughly five or six gallons of fuel—less than two hours of driving time—remained in the vintage car's large gas tank.

"Relax," Charlie hollered back at me with that broad, carefree smile on his face, curly hair whipping away in the breeze. "We're heading west. We'll be there before you know it."

It had been at least six hours, maybe more, since we'd last seen another human being and that had been back at the gas station we had topped off the tank at in a very forgettable three-building town along the road. An hour later, the tree-lined hills had given way to this barren desert, occasionally broken up by clusters of cactus and small scraggily shrubs dotting the small rocky hills and cap rocks.

Looking around, I could see nothing but more of the same for seemingly endless miles in any direction and no sign of any civilization of any kind. Come to think of it, I hadn't even seen so much as a road sign since shortly after we'd left the gas station.

With a last withering look at the fuel gauge and then back again at Charlie, which he predictably and cheerfully ignored, I sat back and was unable to fight off another sigh. We were indeed heading west all right, toward a sun that arced ever closer to the horizon, and that was the general direction we needed to get to our intended destination, Phoenix. But I couldn't help but recall the last such navigational misadventure we had suffered in this very same car.

That time we had been heading for San Antonio when Charlie veered off the planned route in favor of a "great shortcut," sure to get us there two hours faster. Of course, there was a great place to eat along the new route. After a not-so-grand tour of the west Texas plains and its "forest" of oil well derricks, I had finally booted him out from behind the wheel and drove us back to the interstate. Once we had made it back to the four-lane freeway we found ourselves quite a lot closer to El Paso than we were to San Antonio. We'd rolled into San Antonio that night, a full eight hours late, and I had sworn that I'd never again let Charlie drive when he was in the same car with me.

The problem with this area of the American Southwest was that it all looked the same for the most part. I was very sure that we could not have possibly made it all the way to California yet. And I very much doubted that we had wandered far enough south to be back in Texas again or even—God forbid—Mexico. But there was no way to tell if we were still in New Mexico. Or if we had actually crossed the state line over into Arizona at some point in this detour of ours.

It really should have been an easy trip—would have been if we'd simply flown down from Denver to Phoenix in the first place as I had originally planned—but even still by driving the nearly thousand-mile journey in Charlie's car, it should have been a piece of cake. Much easier at least, than the task that awaited us in Phoenix, assuming we would ever get there.

The two of us were to make a presentation on our company's behalf to the city's planning commission to oversee a complete overhaul of the city's entire public transportation system.

Many Arizona companies were vying for the multi-billion-dollar project and it would have seemed to be the logical choice to go with one of the locals. But PGH had a well-earned national reputation for being the best of the best in the country, if not the world, and that just completed project in Minnesota that I mentioned before was still drawing rave reviews from everyone connected to the project. Even its original detractors were grudgingly admitting they couldn't have done it better.

Old Man Pinelli had started the firm decades ago and taken on John Gonzalez and David Hall when neither of his sons showed any interest in following in his footsteps. The rumor mill had it that the Old Man was grooming someone to take his place instead of one of his three sons. I appeared to be the front runner, if you listened to the office gossip.

All I could say was that if that were true, the Old Man hadn't said a word about it to me. But I did have to admit that being the point man for the company like this, and on more than one occasion, made we wonder if the rumors were true after all.

Maybe that's why the old man indulged Charlie on little things like driving this old car to a presentation instead of flying. Maybe that's why I did it too. Even when it led to getting us lost out in the middle of nowhere.

Again.

* * * * *

It took the sun all of ninety minutes to slip the rest of the way down and touch the horizon. The gas gauge needle hovered uncomfortably close to the big E and there still wasn't a building in sight.

"Charlie," I growled.

"What?" he replied and I swear I saw a bright halo appear above his head for a brief moment.

"Charlie!" I snarled.

"Relax, brother," he replied in that insufferably cheerful, happy-go-luck tone of his. "We're fine."

“CHARLIE!!!!” I’m pretty sure I roared it this time.

“See,” he said, looking straight ahead. “What did I tell you? Nothing to worry about, Pete, nothing to worry about at all.”

“Wha….” Was all I could choke out as I looked out beyond the windshield. We were just topping a slight hill and right there in front of us, about a mile ahead and nestled snugly in a very small valley, was the prime example of why my happy-go-lucky friend was also one lucky son of a bitch.

I’m not kidding. I dare you to toss the man into a sewer and I swear that he will step right back out bathed in diamonds, smelling like fresh roses and have a supermodel draped on each arm. No matter how many times you toss him in.

His luck held up again today as out there in the middle of nowhere, surrounded by nothing but scruffy desert bushes and sand, was one of the most remarkable buildings I’d ever seen in my life. The base of the thing would easily cover a New York City block and it stood at least twenty stories tall. The outer walls of smooth, ivory white concrete swept up and away from the core of the building on each side except for what appeared to be the front, giving the building an almost angelic look.

It was all trimmed out in panes of glass and steel and, even now in the fading light of the day, it sparkled and shimmered in ways I'd never seen before in any other building. I was impressed and absolutely jealous of whoever had designed it all at the same time.

"Wow," Charlie said in a tone that implied that he was just as impressed as I was. "She's something else. I wonder what kind of place that is."

"Hard to say," I replied, when I found my voice again. We were still several hundred yards away and there wasn't a sign to be found on the building or anywhere nearby the place. Aside from a very small, and completely empty parking area that could have only held a couple of cars at most, located near what appeared to be the building's main entrance, not a single vehicle could be found around the exterior either. Although, I suppose in a hot desert climate there would be an underground parking area to keep the cars cool and clean of any dust.

The whole scene suddenly struck me as being a little eerie. But the place represented our only chance to find shelter for the night, fuel for our gas-starved tank, as well as an opportunity to find out exactly where we were and to get us back on track for Phoenix in the morning. With me firmly behind the wheel this time, of course, until we got to Phoenix and then back to Denver. Assuming I didn't bail on the whole thing and fly home after we were done.

Charlie pulled off the road and parked a few yards away from the entrance where the first clue to what lay inside rested just above the darkened glass doors. Written in large letters of stainless steel, in a slanted type of block-lettered font, was a single word:

INFINITY

Well, that wasn't much of a help to figuring out what the place was, any more than the reflective windows that kept the interior a mystery to us as we both started to get out of the car. But all that really mattered was that it had to have some way to help us get to where we needed to go. Provided the entrance would open when we stepped up to it. Fortunately, we were spared having to walk up and tap on the glass.

One of the glass panels silently slid open and an older man, decked out in an old-fashioned knee-length forest green topcoat and cap, stepped out to greet us. He reminded me of a doorman at a five-star hotel that I stayed at during my last visit to New York City. Only that man had needed the coat to ward off the freezing New York winter weather outside. As warm as it was out here, I was surprised the old guy even had the coat on. It was somewhat surprising that he wasn't breaking out in a sweat under that thing.

"Gentlemen," he greeted us, as cool as the proverbial cucumber. "Welcome to The Infinity."

"Thanks, glad to be here," I replied, seeing as I was the closest to the man. "What exactly is 'The Infinity?'"

"Why, it's the finest hotel in the country of course, sir," he answered, his tone conveying the 'well duh' quite properly and perfectly. I let it slide out of relief. "It looks like you two could use a room, a good meal and a bath."

"Probably not in that order either," Charlie quipped.

"We could also use some directions to the nearest gas station and the quickest way back to the interstate in the morning," I added.

"Well, we have plenty of fuel here so we'll be happy to fill her up for you when we park it in the garage below," the old man said with a wave of his hand at Charlie to leave the keys in the ignition. "We'll bring your luggage up to your rooms for you as well. Where were you two boys heading?"

"Phoenix," I answered, reaching back for my wallet to tip him, only to have him wave off the gratuity.

"Phoenix," he repeated in a voice barely above that of a whisper even as a strange look quickly passed across his face. "Arising anew from the ashes of destruction."

"Excuse me," I replied, uncertain I'd heard him correctly because what I thought I'd heard really didn't make much sense to me.

"Oh, it was nothing, sir," he replied with a slight smile as he stepped aside to allow Charlie and I to pass by him on the way to the door. "Just an old man's fondness for Greek mythology is all. Go on inside and the front desk will get you all set up for the night and they will have directions ready for you when you are ready to check out."

There seemed to be more to his remark than he had made out and I considered pressing him on the issue, for all of about two seconds. But it had been a very long day and the thought of a good meal, a quick shower and a good night's sleep all too easily trumped my curiosity. So I followed Charlie to the door, which dutifully slid open for us as we approached.

As we crossed the threshold, the temperature difference between the air outside and the air inside the building we entered was slight, but for some odd reason I felt a harsh icy shiver travel the length of my spine as soon as the door slid shut behind me.

TWO

The old man watched the two new arrivals disappear into the darkness beyond the door, which quickly slid shut behind them without a sound. He turned around for a moment to glance over at the vehicle they had arrived in.

"Phoenix indeed," he murmured sadly. "If only…"

He trailed off as he swung his gaze upward and took a long look at the darkening skies above, a few stars already becoming visible.

"Not very long to go now," he said wearily. "If only there was another way…"

Ignoring the car, the keys dangling from the ignition and the luggage still inside the trunk, the old doorman turned back to the building and walked quickly back to the entrance. No sooner had the doors slid closed behind him than the entire building began to shimmer and fade. A few seconds later, a desert hawk soared unimpeded through the very same space where a twenty-story building had just been located, and perched for the long cold night ahead on the only thing left behind—an abandoned 1957 Pontiac Star Chief convertible.

* * * * *

When neither Childress nor Womack arrived for the presentation in Phoenix, a call was made to their firm. Concern grew to alarm when Old Man Pinelli's secretary called the hotel they were booked to stay in and discovered that the pair had failed to check in.

The state police in both Arizona and New Mexico were contacted and missing person reports filed. The desk sergeant in Arizona had tried to put it off as two young men who likely sidetracked to Vegas and lost track of time.

But the Old Man was having none of it. Charlie might, *might*, lose track of time on one of his tangents that the Old Man had found endearing. But not Peter. The laws of the universe would fail before Peter would neglect to keep a commitment, especially one as important as what awaited them in Phoenix. If they had failed to show up, something was terribly wrong.

So great was his concern that the Old Man even pulled some strings, calling in favors with government officials collected over the years, and got the FBI involved in the case. Once word reached the local cops in the southwestern states that the Feds were involved, the disappearance of the two engineers suddenly became a much higher priority.

The planned route the men had taken to get from Denver to Phoenix was being scoured on the ground and from the air. Officials pored over footage from surveillance cameras, looking for any sign of the two men and the very unique vehicle they traveled in.

The biggest concern in the back of everyone's mind, doubly so for the Old Man's, was if the men had met with foul play, they could have been taken anywhere. Then again, one investigator remarked after learning of the driver's propensity for unplanned detours, they could have taken themselves anywhere and gotten themselves good and lost with no clues left behind for the searchers to find them.

* * * * *

Five days after Womack and Childress had pulled up to the Infinity, the vintage car on every cop's hot sheet still sat where Womack had parked it. The keys were still there in the ignition, and the open vehicle had obviously served as temporary nighttime shelter to a variety of the desert's wildlife, when Officer Ray Lucero found it.

The fifteen-year veteran of the New Mexico State Police thoroughly enjoyed patrolling the highways. So much so that he refused to take the sergeant's exam so that he would rise no higher than senior patrolman. Lucero did not want to be pulled out of the patrol car and chained to a desk. In all of those years on the job, just when Lucero had thought he'd seen it all, there was always something new that would come along and remind him why he stayed behind a wheel and far away from driving that loathsome desk.

If one carved the state up into four quarters, then District 3, where Lucero had been assigned when he first joined the NMSP, was located in the southeastern quadrant of the state. They had been briefed on the hot missing persons case that had drawn federal interest even though the two men had last been seen hundreds of miles to the west and should be nowhere near Lucero's district for any reason at all.

The pair, engineers from a firm in Colorado that had several federal contracts, they had been told, was supposed to have arrived in Phoenix four days ago. The last reported sighting of the pair had them at a gas station in Gallup, after having lunch at Granpappy's Old West Grill, some twenty miles from the Arizona state line. The pair, after departing Gallup, should have continued going west for about three hours before turning south at Flagstaff for another three hours to complete their journey on to their destination.

They, and their easily noticeable car, had never arrived at their hotel and hadn't been spotted anywhere along any of the possible routes between Gallup and Phoenix. Because of the D.C. connection, they'd been told, both the FBI and Homeland were hot on the case with agents scouring the countryside across the two states, looking for any sign of the missing men. Even the Mexican authorities had been alerted, in case the men had run afoul of one of the drug cartels that had recently infiltrated the American border.

Being so far to the east, Lucero never dreamed that he would ever be involved in the case. Even when an old friend called him that afternoon and interrupted his lunch break to tell him he'd been flying his two-seater out near Boy Scout Mountain, about an hour west of District 3's headquarters in Roswell, and he'd spotted an abandoned vehicle. It was parked just off State Highway 246 not far from the road that led to the top of the mountain and it looked like the missing car.

"It's an old Pontiac all right, and it looked like it is in great shape for its age," the pilot reported. "I circled around for a while to see if anyone was nearby but there's not a soul out there. I figured you might want to go out and check it out, make sure everything is kosher."

Lucero had thanked him for the call but, figuring it was probably someone out hiking, decided to finish his green chili cheeseburger and coffee before getting into his cruiser for the one-hour drive out to the remote location. He expected to find nothing out there once he arrived.

He was wrong.

"Well, I'll be damned," Lucero swore as he pulled up to the location and saw the 1957 Pontiac Star Chief convertible with Colorado plates that was a perfect match for the BOLO they had received a few days ago. "What the hell are you two idiots doing way out here?"

Not wanting to disturb what likely had the potential to become a major crime scene, Lucero parked the cruiser on the other side of the road. He stepped out and slowly approached the abandoned car, his trained eyes taking in every detail of the scene. It simply made no sense to him for this car to be out here of all places. Even if they had gotten lost, there hadn't been a cloud in the sky for over a week, and between the sun and a nearly full moon for the last few nights, two men smart enough to be successful engineers should have been smart enough to realize they were going the wrong way, simply by watching those two bright objects moving across the open skies.

Nor did it make any sense that this was an intended destination. Aside from it being out in the middle of nowhere, why would they bother going so far west as Gallup only to backtrack hundreds of miles east to arrive out here? And how would they have pulled that off without being seen in this car by someone along the way? They would have needed at least one more stop for fuel somewhere along the road. Nor were there many ways to get out here, and all of the possible roads were pretty well traveled.

As he neared the car, he noticed a set of footprints, obviously the driver's, leading toward the back of the car and around to the passenger side. Carefully avoiding the tracks, Lucero leaned over the door and took a long look around. The car had been here for a few days at least, judging from the dust and assorted animal scat scattered on the seats and the floorboards. The keys were still in the ignition and Lucero, after putting on a pair of latex gloves to avoid leaving his own prints, eased into the driver's seat, engaged the clutch and turned the ignition.

The engine fired right up and the needle on the fuel gauge quickly swung all the way across to the full mark. Turning off the engine, Lucero pulled the keys out as he slipped back out from behind the wheel and walked to the trunk to open it, fully expecting to see one or two bodies lying within.

But all he found were the men's luggage and computer bags. It appeared to him at first glance that nothing was missing from the bags. Perplexed, Lucero closed the trunk and followed the driver's footprints. Whoever had been driving had walked over to the passenger's side, where his tracks joined a second set of prints which could only be those of the other missing man.

The two men had then walked away together, away from both the car and the road, one following right behind the other, only slightly to the left of the lead man, for eight full strides and then the tracks stopped suddenly. Literally in mid-stride it seemed. Lucero scoured the ground within range of even a tall man's stride but he could find no sign of where the next step of the two men had landed.

It was if they'd walked right off the earth. Or perhaps something had swooped in and scooped the pair away before their feet could find solid ground again.

"Aw hell," Lucero swore to himself. They were just close enough to Roswell that if the pair was not found, and quickly at that, every damn alien abduction loon in the country would descend on the area in hordes. Each claiming the pair had been abducted by little gray men or some other lunacy.

Well, the sooner he called this in to his captain and she called the Feds to let them know the car had turned up, the sooner they could hand this headache off to the boys from D.C. and let them deal with it. Lucero turned to walk back to his cruiser but something drew his eyes up to the sky.

"*Madre de Dios*!" Lucero exclaimed, his eyes wide with terror as he started to cross himself. They were the last words, his last act, his last conscious thought, as he failed to complete the cross before a wall of fire that stretched across the horizon engulfed him and the car that no one would ever know had finally been found.

THREE

If we had been impressed by what we'd seen of the exterior of the Infinity, and believe me, we were *very* impressed by that, then we were completely stopped in our tracks by what we saw after we had stepped inside the place.

Literally.

Barely two full steps into what could only be described as a palatial lobby, both Charlie and I stopped cold and just looked around. I had stayed in quite a few hotels, five-star hotels at that mind you, that could have very easily fit inside the main lobby of this place, with room to spare. They must have spent a small fortune just on the front desk area alone.

Like the exterior, the interior was almost completely covered by darkened glass walls framed in stainless steel. The tile floor we walked on had to be made of some of the finest Italian porcelain that I'd ever seen. It was all laid out in a checkerboard pattern of white and forest green with each square trimmed in gold.

The front desk area was similarly constructed, a huge base of stainless steel that seamlessly grew right out of the floor, topped with the gold-trimmed green tile. More of the dark glass served as a back wall with the name of the hotel in stainless steel lettering. Then we both looked up and discovered that we hadn't yet seen the most impressive aspect of the interior.

"Wow," Charlie said in a hushed tone. To be honest with you, I probably couldn't have said it any better than he had.

The ceiling above us was made of crystal clear glass, giving one an unobstructed view of the center tower and the air bridges that connected every floor of the tower on each side to the outer shells of the building's winged walls.

From what I'd seen of the outside, the creatively designed center tower was only about twenty floors in height. But looking up from the inside, it appeared the tower continued on and on into, okay I'll say it, infinity.

So now we knew where the name had come from at least.

But what I really itched to know was who had designed the place. Who had built this incredible structure and, more importantly, how in the world had they managed to do so without everyone in my line of work knowing about it?

"You ever hear of anything like this being put together?" I asked Charlie as I continued to admire the place with more than a touch of envy.

"Nope," Charlie said. "But you'd be more likely to have read about it than I."

That was too true. Trust me, something like this would have made the rounds no matter how hard they tried to keep it secret. And Charlie was right. I would have heard or read about it somewhere since I read every magazine, journal or article related to my line of work. I did more than just read the material. I devoured everything I could get my hands on. It was a habit I'd acquired from my grade school days when a broken leg and two subsequent surgeries confined me to a wheelchair and the school library during recess and lunch break for most of the year.

By the time I was no longer confined to the chair and back on my own two feet again, I was on a first-name basis with the old librarian and had gone through just about every book she had on the shelves. That love of reading had stayed with me through the years. So I was pretty sure that if there had been any publicity about this place I would have read about it.

"They sure do make this place easy on the eyes," Charlie remarked and something in his tone made me look away from the amazing architecture. I looked over in the direction of his line of vision to see what had attracted his attention. But all I saw was a pair of young men, obviously hotel employees, dressed in a similar style as the old man we'd met outside, minus the heavy topcoat.

Each man had matching tailored outfits of silver-gray vests, slacks and shoes with forest green ties and long-sleeved white shirts. It was an interesting combination of modern and turn-of-the-twentieth-century style that lent a sense of elegance and class. While they looked quite good, they were hardly Charlie's style. But before I could ask him about potential latency, the two men moved off toward the elevators, no longer blocking my view of what had actually caught Charlie's eye.

The young woman was also a member of the hotel staff. Like the two men, she had a nametag pinned over the left breast of her garment, but that was where the similarities in uniform style ended. Her uniform was a green-and-white, low-cut halter top trimmed in gold with a small diagonal slash of gold separating the two colors in the front over a silver-gray miniskirt.

The outfit wasn't gaudy or sleazy at all and managed to add to the overall feel of high class that permeated the place. But it still managed to present a rather splendid display of bosom and thigh, guaranteed to warm even the coldest of hearts.

And this young, ginger beauty certainly had it to display.

"I see why it is called Infinity," Charlie said, taking a step in the young lady's direction. "That's just about the right amount of time I'd like to spend here."

"Hold on a minute, Romeo," I said, putting a hand on his shoulder. "Let's get checked into a room first. Then you can go introduce yourself."

About then, Charlie made eye contact with her and damned if the glances and body language flying between the two all but set the time and place that they would meet up after we got settled in.

Have I mentioned yet that the insufferably lucky son of a bitch was a walking babe magnet?

With a shake of my head, I steered him toward the front desk after he'd managed to get close enough for both of us to read her nametag. It turned out that the latest love of Charlie's life was named Carrie and he, his plans for the evening obviously set, was in full goofy smile face mode by the time we got to the desk. I just wanted a room with a bed, some food and a good road map with maybe an hour or two of exploring this amazing place thrown in for good measure.

Then a woman with long, raven-black hair and looking every bit as lovely as Charlie's Carrie in her uniform stood across from us on the other side of the desk. At that very moment, I found myself conceding that maybe Charlie's explanation for the hotel's name origins might have been a little more on the mark than mine.

"Good evening, gentlemen," she greeted us, her nametag identifying her as Liz. "Welcome to Infinity. How can I help you?"

It had never happened to me before, I swear, but when I opened my mouth to answer her, not a sound came out. Out of the corner of my eye, I caught a smirk forming on Charlie's face and shot him an annoyed "later for you, buddy" look before returning my attention back to Liz and tried answering her again. Fortunately, this time around, the vocal chords decided to work.

"Yes, my crack navigator here," I nodded in Charlie's direction, "got us good and lost. It has been a very long day and we'd like to check in, if there's anything available."

"One room or two?" she asked.

"Separate rooms," I answered. I may love the guy like a brother but I'd spent enough time with him for one day, thank you very much. "On the same floor if possible, but definitely separate rooms."

"Of course," she said with an understanding smile and produced a pair of stainless steel room keys. Each had a dark green stripe running down one side and green numbers on the other. The backs of the cards were unmarked.

"These the room numbers?" Charlie asked as he took one of the cards, a finger pointing at the four-digit number.

"Yes," she answered.

"Excellent. Catch up with you later, Pete," Charlie said as he all but sprinted away from the desk in search of Carrie.

"Hey, Charlie," I exclaimed, little good it did me. He never so much as looked back as he exited the lobby and disappeared into the main area of the hotel.

"Well," I said with a sigh as I pulled out my wallet, "as usual it looks like I get stuck with the check."

I withdrew the company credit card, and that at least was the one thing the Old Man didn't trust Charlie with, without bothering to ask how much this stay would cost. Judging by the looks of it, this wouldn't be a cheap bill. But I figured since the Old Man's penchant for letting Charlie get us into these situations was as equally to blame as Charlie himself, then the Old Man owed us an expensive night out. Maybe the sticker shock on the monthly bill would convince him that flying us to these things was the better option whenever Charlie's driving was concerned. Then again, as much money as the two of us had made the firm over the years, he would probably most likely let it slide without a word. Either way, I wasn't about to feel the least bit guilty over the expense. I probably wouldn't take it easy on the room service tab either, come to think of it.

"No need for that, sir," Liz said when I handed her the card. "Payment is settled at checkout. All we need for now is your names."

"Really?" I said in disbelief as I put the card back in my wallet and picked up my key to get a look at the room number. "Well, my fleet-footed friend who took off with his room key is Charlie Womack. And the occupant of Room 4264 is Peter Childress."

"Very good, Mr. Childress," she replied, tapping in our names on the keyboard set into the tiled countertop and then handed me a brochure. "You're all set for the night.

Don't hesitate to let us know if you need anything. There is detailed map inside that will show you how to get to your room and around the hotel as well."

"Thank you. Oh, how soon will our luggage be brought up?"

"Everything you need will be in your room shortly, Mr. Childress," she replied, and for a second, I wondered if I had caught a strange undertone to the way she had said that. But I shook it off as my being tired and let it slide.

"Excellent. Thank you," I said and turned away to head for the elevator while opening the brochure. After a few steps, I remembered that we still needed directions to get back to the interstate. I turned back around to ask her, only to find the front desk deserted. She had disappeared somewhere although I couldn't see any possible door near enough for her to have escaped that quickly. Come to think of it, I hadn't really noticed where she had come *from* when we first got to the desk.

"Is there something I can help you with, young man?" said a deep baritone voice behind me.

I turned around to find myself facing a kindly looking older man with a receding hairline above a pair of thin gold-rimmed glasses and a salt and pepper beard that gave him something of a grandfatherly appearance. The pleasant smile on his face did not quite reach the sad eyes behind the glasses. He had a tablet in his hand, a model I'd not seen at any Best Buy, and his nametag simply identified him as 'Manager" and nothing more. Unlike the other male employees I'd seen, he was clad in a standard cut dark green suit with only his silver-gray shirt providing the only break in the color.

"Yeah, my friend and I got ourselves good and lost and only stumbled on this place by accident," I explained. "I was hoping to get some directions back to the interstate."

"And civilization?" he added.

"Well, I suppose," I answered a little shame faced. "Although I suspect civilization comes up a little short when compared to this place. How many people can you fit in here?"

"We do try," he said, smiling a little to show no offense had been taken. "We'll make sure we'll get you headed in the right direction before you're ready to leave here. As for capacity, we're nearly at full capacity now and we have just under six thousand guests. In the meantime, I hope you'll take advantage of the amenities and fully enjoy your stay with us."

"I will," I replied, thinking of exploring the place as much as possible and maybe even coming back this way on the return drive home, especially if the presentation in Phoenix went well. "Six thousand capacity? Whew, that's more than a few towns I've lived in. I'd love to know how the place was built. It pretty much puts anything I've ever designed to shame."

"You're in construction then?"

"I design major civil projects," I said with more than just a little hint of pride. "Mostly metro transit hubs—subways, elevated trains and buses—and this really huge multi-use sports complex over in Texas too. But I've never come up with anything in the same league as this place. It's amazing."

"Well, thank you," the manager replied. "Maybe we can find some information on how it was built for you to look over. I'll send it up to your room shortly."

"Thanks," I said before adding jokingly as I turned away to head for the elevator. "If I'm not careful, I could spend an eternity here just studying this place."

"Well, hopefully it won't take you quite that long to sort it out," he said and I thought I caught an odd undertone in his voice. Either it was the company way for the employees or I must be pretty tired. "Good evening, Mr. Childress."

I was in the elevator with the doors closed before it struck me that he hadn't asked for my room number. He also knew my name without being introduced. On another day, I might have worried over the problem a little, but I was too tired from the day to sort it out. Besides, the man's tablet was no doubt synced to the hotel's system and he probably had access to everything that happened under the roof of this place, no matter how big that roof was. No, all that was on my mind was a shower, a change of clothes and a meal.

And yet, even as I studied the map in the brochure, all I kept seeing was a mysterious raven-haired woman whom I had only just met.

FOUR

The manager studied the tablet intently, keeping track of Childress' progress toward the elevators from the corner of his eye. Only when Childress was in the elevator cab with the doors firmly closed behind him did the manager finally look fully up. He simply stared at the shiny closed doors, completely lost in thought.

At first glance, he had to admit, Childress certainly showed some promise. But there had been far too many others that had walked into this lobby that had also shown similar promise. Getting his hopes up once again, only to have those hopes cruelly dashed as they had before when they had all failed to deliver. There simply couldn't be many more options to choose from out there. They were so very near capacity now; maybe the time had finally come after all.

The manager had never been a praying man, especially earlier in his life. Though lately, he had to admit, he was becoming more and more tempted to take up the practice. The problem, as he saw it, was that if he started praying to any of the deities known to mankind—or even all of them—he might just get an answer.

Worse still, he would probably find that said answer would not be to his liking at all.

No. It was better for him to sit back, continuing to wait patiently, while at the same time keeping a close eye on young Mr. Childress and let events play out as they would. He could not, under any circumstances whatsoever, attempt to force the issue. That way lay absolute disaster. So, after a few quick taps on the tablet, he tucked it between his arm and his chest and briskly walked toward the front desk.

Stepping around behind the desk's back wall, where a passageway lay hidden from view, the manager quickly made his way up a flight of stairs that led to his office. The potential of the newly arrived Mr. Childress notwithstanding, there was still plenty of work for him to do.

But, as he sat down at his desk, he found himself fighting down a very strong urge to get right back up out of his chair, march straight for Room 4264 and, as the old saying in these parts went, lay all of his cards on the table. Consequences be damned. It took every ounce of the self-discipline learned over a long lifetime, to fight down the compulsion and remain seated at his desk. But even then, it had been a very, very close thing.

* * * * *

Unknown to both of the men, there had been another set of eyes watching their brief discussion with keen interest. Not even the manager himself was aware that the letter 'T' in the hotel's name displayed behind the front desk also served as a doorway to a small storage room within the wall. One person had discovered it though, soon after her arrival and posting to her position behind the front desk, and she had kept her discovery a very closely guarded secret. It suited her greatly, and for more than one reason, to have this quiet place serve her as a sanctum. From this place, she could safely observe and consider her situation free from the fear of discovery.

For very much like her manager, Liz also awaited the arrival of a specific type of guest. She too had seen a few possible candidates come and go over time, but her motivations were nothing like the manager's. She too had gotten her hopes up on more than one occasion, only to have them just as quickly dashed. And she too had taken quick notice of Mr. Childress, even though she could not say exactly what it was about him that had so attracted her attention so quickly.

But when the chance presented itself for her to slip into the cubby hole and observe him unnoticed, she hadn't hesitated to do so for even a second. Standing on the other side of the 'T,' holding it slightly ajar so as to allow her to look out, she watched the manager closely. She'd been around him long enough now to read his facial expressions so well that she could follow the conversation even though she was well out of earshot.

She watched intently as the conversation quickly wrapped up and the two men parted company. Childress headed off to the elevators, obviously heading for his room. She had long ago prepared his room especially for the arrival of someone she would require assistance from. The manager, after watching Childress enter the elevator, was clearly heading up to his office. She listened as he ascended the stairs and closed the office door before she straightened her uniform and stepped back out to the front desk.

Yes, she affirmed to herself, the manager had indeed also taken special notice of the latest arrival. All that remained to be seen now was if Peter Childress was the man they had both been waiting for. That and, of course, which one of them would get to him first when they knew for sure he was the one they sought.

"Liz?"

She was shaken out of her musings by one of the room attendants holding a tan leather billfold out to her from the other side of the desk.

“I found this lying on the ground near the guest lounge,” the man said. “I think it belongs to one of the guests.”

“Of course, Kenny,” Liz answered, taking the wallet and flipping it open for identification. “It looks like it belongs to Mr. Womack. He just checked in a few minutes ago. I’ll call his room and let him know that we have it down here. Thank you.”

Kenny, who had at one time been an early candidate that she had kept an eye on, cheerfully went on his way to tend to his duties while she dropped the wallet into a drawer. As she picked up the phone to leave Mr. Womack a message—she doubted she would catch him in his room—she wondered what the manager’s next move would be and what, if anything, she should do about it.

FIVE

I had fully expected to find someone seated on a chair in the elevator cab and asking me what floor I wanted to go to. I'd been to a hotel or two that still had that kind of setup in place. There was even an old hotel in New Mexico, where the old Hollywood movie stars would stay while filming the old black-and-while westerns, where one had to call the front desk to have them run over to the elevator and bring it up to the desired floor. But not only wasn't there an operator in the cab, even the standard panel with several rows of numbered buttons was missing.

Instead, I got a small panel with a speaker grille seated below a six-digit LCD display that currently read: Ground. Between the display and the grille was a card slot. As soon as the doors closed, a very pleasant baritone voice emitted from the speaker.

"Insert room key card please."

I slipped my card into the slot, the display changed to 4264 and up we went to the fourth floor as quickly and as smoothly as any elevator I'd ever ridden in. The doors silently parted, I collected my key card and stepped out of the car.

"Room 4264 is located on the Main Tower Corridor to your right, Mr. Childress," instructed the elevator voice from behind me and then the doors closed. I was impressed that their system put an occupant's name to a new room so quickly and incorporated that information in such a small, but extremely customer friendly way. The door to my left was numbered 4299 and the first door to the right was 4200. Looking down the long corridor, I wondered how long a walk I had to go to get to my room. Then I got a better look at the corridor.

I should have known.

A moving walkway ran along the outer wall of the corridor, opposite of the rooms, obviously intended to help tired guests get to their room with a minimum of expended effort. Stepping onto the moving belt without losing my balance wasn't so hard to do. I had a feeling this would be the first of many more surprises that I would discover about this place.

The walkway's easy pace was such as to allow an easy access and egress. It also gave me time to take in the fact that they hadn't taken the cheap route when it came to the hallway décor either. As I kept track of the numbers on the passing room doors, it came to me that the rooms must not be all that large based on the distance between the doors. It would likely be nothing more than just a bed and a small bath, like some of the hotels in Tokyo I'd read about a few years back. It didn't take that long for my door to come into view and I easily stepped onto the tiled floor, waved the key card in front of what appeared to be the card reader on the right side of the door and stepped on in.

My condo back in Denver, which was far from small, could have easily fit inside this room and that didn't include the bathroom and closet area in the rear of the room.

"Sure," I muttered aloud with a shake of my head as I took it all in. "Why the hell not."

The room was done in the hotel's green and silver-gray color scheme, of course, and everything was large although how they worked it out to be this huge within the apparent available space escaped me. From the king-sized bed to the walk-in closet where my now empty suitcase sat on the floor below my clothing, either hung on the rack or folded neatly on the shelves. How the valet had figured out which bags were mine and not Charlie's was impressive, but not nearly as impressive as the bathroom. Nearly as large as my living room at home, it had a huge bathtub and a separate shower with a large overhead in-ceiling showerhead above that looked to be capable to match a heavy thunderstorm in downpour capacity.

A large work desk, complete with my computer bag resting atop it, sat beneath a picture window next to a rear room exit against the far wall, giving a great view of what looked to be a huge indoor park—filled with green grass, trees, bushes and even a small lake and air without even the slightest hint of having been circulated—beyond the window.

I opened the rear door and stepped outside onto a small patio area that appeared to be standard for every room on the level. The main tower had a hollow center and, as I had seen back in the main lobby, and when I looked up I could see floor levels that seemingly stretched ever upward without any apparent ceiling. The view enjoyed of the massive park here on this level from any of the floors above must be quite spectacular.

That tears it, I decided right there, Charlie would drop me off here on the way back to Denver. I had a few weeks of vacation time coming and I would spend them right here so I could really give this place a good looking over. First off, I would find the person who created this fantastic place and shamelessly bow to the grand master. Then I would just as shamelessly steal every design idea that I could work out and incorporate it in just about everything I designed in the future. The ability to take a finite amount of space and somehow make it appear to border on the infinite was nearly beyond comprehension.

I stepped back into the room and only then noted the absence of a standard hotel room appliance—a television. Then again, with what this place had to offer, I suppose encouraging a guest to be a couch potato glued to the TV screen would be counter-productive. I for one, I can assure you, wouldn't miss the boob tube for a second.

But what I was missing, I realized as I was unpacking my computer bag, was the satchel with our presentation materials stored inside. I had wanted to go over it all one final time the night before our arrival for the presentation in Phoenix, a half hour or so of work squeezed around exploring this grand palace tonight. I assumed that they had probably delivered the material to Charlie's room instead of mine, which ordinarily would not have been a problem, except for one little detail. Charlie had grabbed his room key and quickly took off before I had been able to catch the room number he had been given. Nor had I thought to ask the woman at the desk where she had put him. It wasn't a problem that a quick call to the front desk wouldn't easily solve.

Providing, of course, that there was a phone to be found anywhere in the room, which there wasn't. Not even in the bathroom, a hotel quirk I had run into and that had annoyed me in the past. Who the hell made phone calls while doing their business on the porcelain throne? Now, I'd pay a little extra to have a phone stashed in there. After a minute or so of scouring the room for any form of communication with the front desk, I abandoned the search and started for the door.

"Whoever heard of a hotel room without a television or phone?" I muttered aloud as I reached for the handle to open the door.

"Call mode activated. State room number to call."

I looked up at the ceiling where the disembodied voice had seemed to have originated from and there in the light fixture was a panel similar to what I'd seen in the elevator.

"I don't know which room I need to call," I said to the empty air.

"Shall I connect you with the front desk?"

"Um, no, that won't be necessary," I answered. It wasn't that urgent a matter and if I didn't run into Charlie soon, I'd try the front desk then. "Never mind. I don't suppose you could tell me why there isn't a television in the room by any chance?"

I wasn't really expecting an answer but I got a reminder of why I was wrong whenever I thought I'd seen everything, at least while staying in this particular hotel. The large window in the rear wall went from clear to black. A menu appeared on what was now a very nice eighty-inch flat screen.

"There are several entertainment channels and games available," the voice informed me. "Unfortunately the live news feed is unavailable at this time. We apologize for the inconvenience and hope to have the issue resolved shortly."

"Thanks, that's okay. I'll try again later. And I can wait on the call as well, thank you."

The window returned to its clear state and the small blue light in the ceiling winked out. I decided to text Charlie for his room number and to see if I could get the satchel from him later on. But when I pulled my cell phone out of my pocket, I was greeted with the no service found message. Well, so much for that idea.

But oddly enough, that little flaw in what had seemed to be the endless perfection of this place gave me some comfort. It was just a little too weird for everything to work this flawlessly, no matter how much time, money and effort had gone into making this place as perfect as possible.

With nothing else pressing for me to do, I decided to grab a quick shower and a change of clothes before going out and doing a little exploring. Once the dirt of the day was washed away and I was freshly attired, the first order of business was one of the sky bridges and the outer shell. Eschewing the moving walkway, I strolled along a few yards further down the corridor until I came to the first sky bridge. There was a tiled break in the moving walkway to allow a pedestrian to step onto the bridge from either the walkway or the corridor without having to be an accomplished acrobat.

The bridge itself spanned a gap of about fifty feet between the central tower and the outer shell and once across, I was confronted with a sign identifying my location as the Outer Fourth Floor. Much like it had been in the corridor in the tower, numbered doors lined in each direction as far as the eye could see. The doors on the right started at 4000 and moved up. To the left the last door was numbered 4199.

Three hundred rooms on one single level. Stepping back onto the bridge so I could look up through the glass-topped dome of the bridge, I still saw what looked like an infinite number of levels that more than exceeded my estimate of twenty stories from the outside.

I did the math in my head. The manager had said they were at near capacity with six thousand guests and giving each guest a room of their own at 300 rooms per level came out to just about twenty floors for guest rooms. Looking up though the dome, it sure seemed to me that there were quite a few more than twenty levels sitting up there.

Well, there was one sure way to find out just how many there actually were. Heading back to the tower, I rode the walkway back around to the elevator, stepped in and instead of sliding in my card as I did not want to go back to my room, I announced my room destination as 6019—adding four to the first number of the current year. It was just as good a number as any other for this little experiment of mine.

It didn't seem to take too long to climb those eighteen stories and when the doors opened, the helpful cab voice announced that Room 6019 could be accessed by taking the walkway to the first sky bridge to the right. Sure enough, the door numbers to the right here in the tower started at 6200. The walkway efficiently deposited me at the sky bridge and I took all of three steps onto it before looking up.

I immediately wished I hadn't done so.

Because here on what should have been the twenty-second floor of the Infinity Hotel, I found myself looking up at what appeared to be an endless stack of levels both in the tower and the outer shell. I looked down and saw more of the same. Turning around, I quickly got back onto the walkway and back into the elevator. It took the cab two patient tries before I managed to respond to its destination request.

"Room 10201."

A pause, a brief sensation of movement and the doors opened. This time I walked to the sky bridge, past the doors with their five-digit numbering that all began with the number ten. I kept my eyes straight and level as I walked out onto the bridge. A quick look up. Another look down. Endless levels in both directions.

I ran back to the elevator this time.

"Room destination?" the voice asked when I failed to slide in my key card.

"30201."

The doors opened. There I saw Room 30201 on the right as I shakily walked over to the sky bridge and looked up. There were still more floors as far as the eye could see and the same was true when I looked down. Stunned, I headed back to the elevator, unsure of how many times I repeated the sequence. The next thing I knew I was standing in the cab, the doors were open and I was staring in numbed shock at a door with the number 150201 in shiny lettering on it. I didn't even bother walking over to the sky bridge this time around. I knew I'd just see more of what I had seen at every previous stop before.

"New destination," I whispered hoarsely as I stepped back into the cab. "Front desk."

The doors slid shut and I could feel the cab dropping and, all too suddenly it seemed to me, considering we had dropped a hundred fifty floors, the doors slid open again to reveal the front lobby. I'd been in the Twin Towers as a young boy, before they had been destroyed in 2001, and it had taken a lot longer for us to get back down from the top of those buildings and they weren't more than two thirds as tall as the height I had reached here. Yet, in just seconds, I had dropped at least one hundred and fifty stories—maybe even more for all I really knew.

Something wasn't right here and either it was with this hotel or it was my mind slipping toward insanity. At the moment it was fifty, fifty on which was the right answer.

Rattled, I slowly stepped out into the lobby and made my way toward the front desk to find the same woman who had checked us in. I am sure that I was as pale as the white tiles below my feet. I wouldn't even want to know what the expression on my face looked like.

"Is there something I can help you with, Mr. Childress?" she asked as I stepped up to the desk.

Sure, sweetheart, you can tell me what the hell is going on around here because there is something seriously wrong about this shiny hotel of yours, I thought to myself. Suddenly all of the perfection that I had marveled at earlier had become frighteningly ominous. What made it even more disconcerting was that I could not say exactly why it had.

There was simply no way any engineering or design sleight of hand could fit one hundred and fifty stories inside what I had seen as a twenty-story building on the outside. And there was no way the building that I had looked at from the outside was even a single foot higher than twenty stories. No matter how long and draining the day had been before we had arrived, I could not possibly have misjudged the building's height by that much. At some point during my ascent, the feeling had sunk in that there was something alien, almost evil, about the entire place and that if I did not get out and very soon, that I would be hopelessly trapped here.

The feeling brought back an unpleasant memory, a series of nightmares I'd suffered through years ago. I would be walking along a long hallway, or between long rows of bookshelves and occasionally a deep, wide-open cavern.

All would be well right up until the point when I'd find my path blocked by a solid wall of some sort. Unconcerned, I would turn around to go back the way I'd came, only to find myself face to face with the obstruction. No matter how I turned, the obstruction was there until I could no longer move, no longer see, no longer breathe…

And then I would wake up, bolting up to a sitting position in bed with my heart pounding in my chest and gasping for air. It had taken the help of a good friend who knew how to interpret dreams; it turned out my subconscious tried to get my attention about a work-related issue, and how to control the things happening in the dream so as to put an end to them.

But this was no dream state. This was a harsh reality that I wanted no part of and there was no friend handy to help guide me away to safety. Well, maybe there was one after all.

"Yes," I replied to Liz's inquiry after what must have been an eternity. "Yes, you can help me. My friend took off rather suddenly and I don't know which room he's staying in. I think one of my bags wound up in his room by mistake and I'd like to get it."

"No problem, Mr. Childress," she said, looking down at the desk for a moment. "He's in Room 11409."

"Thank you," I said, turning to go back to the elevator even as a large part of me really wanted no part of that cab ever again.

"But he's not in his room right now," she called out after me. "He's yet to use his card to access the room. It looks like he is currently in the casino."

The casino made sense; he'd head straight off to play in a place like this. Okay, so the plan was to collect Charlie, get our luggage, find his car and get us the hell out of here. And if the damn thing was still out of gas when we located it, then I'd push it all the way to Phoenix if I had to. Which left just one simple question: How do I get to the garage? I didn't remember seeing the garage on the map.

"You can get to the casino through the guest lounge," Liz said in response to what must have been the questioning look on my face. "It is to the left and just at the top of the steps."

Okay, so that was the other question that I should have been thinking about asking her. As for the aforementioned garage....

"Thank you," I replied. "By the way, if that bag isn't in his room, it will probably still be in our car. How do you get down to the garage from here?"

"Oh, I'm afraid guest access to the garage isn't allowed," she answered. "The way things are stored down there it really isn't safe unless you know where you're going. Just let us know and we'll have someone see if the bag is down there and have them bring it up to you."

I'm not a paranoid man by nature, any more than I am given to panic attacks, but this place had a way of getting in my head that I didn't much care for at all. I found myself thinking that there was more than just 'guest safety' involved in not wanting me to get to our car. Okay then. Plan B. Get to Charlie and get the hell outside. Try to get a cell signal and if that didn't work, then start walking down the damn road.

“Will do,” I said as I walked toward the lounge to fetch Charlie, shooting a quick glance over at the darkened glass entrance where we’d come in earlier.

Which was now nothing more than a solid stainless steel wall that was completely bare of a single window or door of any kind. Various types of artwork hung across its face and several pieces of furniture were scattered in front of it. But not a single exit, of any construction, was there to be found. I stopped dead in my tracks, again, and wondered how many more shocks would it take before my heart just said screw this insanity and quit beating any longer.

“Mr. Childress?”

“Wasn’t there a door to the outside over there when we came in?” I asked her without turning my head.

“A door?” she replied. “No, Mr. Childress, that wall has been there just like that ever since we opened the hotel.”

Lie! I knew for a fact that the entrance had been right there when we came in. But shouting “Liar. Liar. Pants on Fire” at the woman wouldn’t do me any good. So it was on to Plan… whatever one I was down to by now. Just get to Charlie. Together we’d surely find a way out of here. But, first things first and that meant finding Charlie.

Get. To. Charlie.

I staggered over to the lounge, turned left and ascended the six carpeted steps to the top and headed for the entryway to the casino, which was filled with dozens of gambling guests. The place would have put even the best Vegas casino to shame and would have easily fit any two Vegas casinos inside its walls. Of course.

How in the hell would I find Charlie in there?

#

SIX

There had been a fleeting moment when Liz would have tried to tell the hotel's newest guest everything that he so desperately needed to know. But before she could even utter a single word, she had spotted the manager out of the corner of her eye, quietly watching them from the walkway atop the solid wall that Childress thought had once been the main entrance. In reality, it actually had been when he had first arrived, but no longer. The manager gave Childress his very careful attention and he could have easily heard every word that passed between her and the target of their mutual interest.

Bitterly disappointed, she held back and instead answered the questions just the way she'd been expected to in her role as the hotel's dutiful front desk clerk. Her outward appearance remained calm, of course, but inwardly she seethed at the missed opportunity. Something had greatly disturbed this new arrival, in a way she had never seen before in any guest, and he was now suddenly seeing the hotel in a different light. Was it enough to suit her purposes? This she did not know any more than if the manager had also noticed the change in him.

She didn't dare explore what that event had been with him, not at this moment with the manager hovering so closely nearby. So instead, she watched Childress walk away and did everything she could to give the impression to those closely watching eyes above that everything was going along just as it should be, that she had not been aware of anything amiss, nor that she was even aware that the manager watched her. Her fingers quickly tapped on the clear keyboard inlaid into the counter in front of her, calling up the log for Childress' key card. The complex system that kept track of every card inside the hotel showed him entering his room, exiting a few short minutes later and returning to the elevator before making his way in several jumps upward through the tower.

He went as far up as that! she thought to herself in shock even as she fought to keep any sign of reaction off her face. Her heart raced then and she reminded herself not to get her hopes up too soon. Still, he had gone that far up the tower and came back down in an obvious state of shock. She knew there could only be one possible explanation as to why he had reacted that way.

Now it was just a matter of her finding a way to speak with him unobserved, to steer him in the direction she desperately needed him to go, and she had a very good idea of how she would do just that. Crafting her most carefully neutral look upon her face, she casually stepped out from behind the desk and headed for the staff office behind the elevators. *Just another staff member carrying out her duties, Mr. Manager,* she thought silently in the direction of the watching man above. *Nothing at all out of the ordinary to see down here, sir.*

* * * * *

As it turned out, Liz needn't have worried about her outward demeanor at all. For the manager was completely focused on Childress alone. He too had called up, and fully reviewed, the tracking data showing where Childress had visited since obtaining his room key card. And the manager too, like Liz, had felt almost an electric charge surging through him as the realization of what Childress' trek through the tower might mean for him.

The manager paid no attention to Liz as she departed the front lobby area and kept it focused solely on the pad in his hand as it tracked the new guest making his way through the hotel. While he'd had his hopes for the man from the start, he was forced to admit that he hadn't expected Childress to have such an extreme reaction to whatever it was that he had discovered quite this quickly. Even when factoring in Childress' professional background.

Something had affected the latest arrival dramatically, of that there was no doubt, but the manager was at a complete loss at what the triggering event could have been. Childress had gone to his room, obviously exhausted from a long and adventurous day, and then for some unknown reason, had walked right back out of his room and worked his way upward in the elevator.

What had he seen to make him do that? *What had he seen?* What was it that had sent him back down here looking for the exit nearly in a state of panic, which seemed an unlikely state for a person like him to easily slip into in the first place? Perhaps, the manager mused, he should track the man down and just ask him flat out? If he did, would Childress tell him? And if he did provide an answer, could that answer be believed?

More importantly to his ultimate goal, would even just the act of asking that question complete and catastrophically undo everything that had been accomplished here so far? Would it render the ultimate goal as forever unattainable and would all of the time spent here have all been for nothing?

The manager sighed in deep frustration, wishing with all of his being that the person responsible for constructing this hotel and everything connected to the matter at hand could provide him with the guidance he so desperately needed right at that minute. But he knew all too well that person would have no helpful answers to provide him.

He knew this because he was that very answerless person.

SEVEN

There had to be hundreds of people milling about inside the casino, maybe even over a thousand or two as far as I could tell once I had worked my way further inside, enough to take a really good look around. I could wander around the place for hours and probably never come close to finding the one person I was looking for.

It was as palatial as the rest of the hotel had been, decked out in marble of green, gold and white on the floors and walls. Gaming tables, cloaked in what appeared to be red velour from my vantage point and surrounded by players of every known game of chance, lay scattered in no identifiable pattern across the vast room. There were even a number of games that I did not recognize at all but they all seemed to not be wanting for action from the guests.

I wandered over to the closest table, the game turned out to be baccarat, and looked over the shoulders of a middle-aged Japanese couple who seemed to be doing quite well, judging by the stacks of chips in front of them.

Come to think of it, as I glanced over the entire table, all six players seated there were getting along very well too.

A squeal of delight brought my attention back to the couple I stood behind. The woman had won a huge hand with a natural nine. The dealer slid over a large pile of chips toward the winner. They apparently decided to get out while they were well ahead, a decision not many were smart enough to make when their luck was running that hot, and gathered up their chips as they jumped out of the green velvet chairs.

"Quitting while you're ahead?" I said to the male companion as he turned away from the table.

"Ha," he replied with a grin. "We would stay here all night the way the cards are falling. But my wife and I must leave early in the morning. My shipping business in Hiroshima is booming and I have an important meeting I cannot miss. We have a very good chance to land a major supply contract with the central government."

"Well," I said as I stepped out of the way so they could head over to the cashier to cash in their chips. "I can see why you have to get up early. You do have a way to go to get home."

"Oh, it isn't that far," the woman, who I assumed was his wife, said. "We'll be home before we know it."

I didn't know the exact mileage, but Arizona to Hiroshima, Japan had to be a good five to six thousand miles and even the fastest plane or private jet would take at least half a day to make the trip. I'd hardly call that getting home before they knew it, but allowing for the exhilaration of having made a killing at the gaming table, I let the remark pass as I watched them walk away.

Returning my attention to the problem at hand, I checked my cell phone again for lack of any better idea of how to track down Charlie and was not really that surprised to find that it still had no signal.

Defeated, I stood there near the casino entrance with no clue what my next step should be. I did not want to leave this place without Charlie in tow. But at some point if I didn't find him, I would have to turn my attention to finding the exit and getting help from the outside. I was still puzzling out the vanishing exit trick. Was there a second lobby, perhaps a floor above the main entrance that I had mistakenly gone to? Aside from there not being any logical reason for such a setup, how could the same woman be stationed at both desks, separated by at least one floor?

Lost in thought, and with absolutely no answers presenting themselves to my rattled brain, I suddenly caught a whiff of meat, clearly broiling over an open flame nearby, and the wonderful aroma of it reminded me that I hadn't eaten in hours. A fact supported by the growling that suddenly began in the pit of my stomach. Maybe some food and a few minutes of quiet thought might be in order here. If nothing else, I could clear my head and my thinking while quieting the rumbling now increasing in earnest in my stomach.

I followed the mouth-watering smells down a short corridor that separated the lounge from the casino and soon found myself in a nearly empty restaurant tastefully done up in a retro 1950s motif. I claimed one of the smaller tables and had barely sat down in the chair before the waitress appeared. I'd seen the old movies and TV shows of the 1950s and I didn't recall any waitresses of the time being dressed quite so, well let's say as close to au naturel as one could get without being arrested for indecent exposure outside of a strip club.

"What can I get for you, hon?" she asked in a throaty Southern accent and in a tone that, along with the way she leaned down toward me to offer a full view of the menu, had this been back home in Denver and I hadn't been in the middle of a complete nervous breakdown, would have likely led us to the nearest bedroom.

Hey, I said I was having a breakdown, I didn't say I was dead and she certainly had it to display. It seemed to be a requirement for employment here.

"Just black coffee," I replied. "And a hamburger, medium well please."

"Sure thing, hon," she said with a knowing wink as she headed off to turn in my order.

A few minutes later, after the burger and coffee had arrived and been quickly dispatched, I felt a little more like myself. I was still convinced that what I had seen and felt earlier was real, but at least I wasn't on the verge of curling up into a fetal position anytime soon. After trying to pay for my meal, only to find out that it had already been billed to my room and I could settle up at checkout, I decided that getting back to our rooms in hopes of finally finding Charlie was still my best move. After securing him, I could then resume my quest to find a way out of here for both of us. Hopefully, by the time I accomplished that, they would have filled up the tank with gas, otherwise we wouldn't get very far. Rising up from my seat, I caught a snippet of conversation from another couple that had been seated two tables away from me.

"You'll simply love London, Annie," the man said, with a Scottish accent, as the couple sat over their dessert.

"Harry's meeting us there in the morning and give us the grand tour. Then it is on to Paris for us both. He's got us on a DC-4 they just converted from military service for passenger flights between London and Paris. We'll be on his company's first flight."

"I can hardly wait, Sean," his companion replied in a matching accent. They were both attired in an older style of clothing, something that seemed to me to predate the 1950s setting. Even the hairstyles had an old feel to them, like the ones in the old black-and-white films from the 30s and 40s, even though neither one of the pair appeared to be any older than I was. "But it hasn't been that long since the war ended. Do you think there's still a lot of damage they haven't fixed up just yet? I hope they've restored the Luvre and returned all of that stolen art."

"No worries, luv," Sean replied. "We'll go back as many times as you like until you've seen everything there, no matter how much the Jerrys stole."

Okay now, there's such a thing as taking this roleplaying stuff too far. Dressing up in the style of an era was one thing, but pretending to actually live in that era to this extent while out in a public setting, aside from some type of convention I suppose, was quite another thing.

"It'll be fine," Sean continued to assure Annie. "You'll see. We can't be but a couple of hours' drive from London. There is just no way I had gotten us that lost last night."

I had walked past their table by then but that last remark stopped me cold in my tracks. Suddenly, they didn't sound like they were acting a part to me any longer and they were here in this hotel after having gotten lost, just like Charlie and I. A part of me very much wanted to just keep on walking away to find Charlie. It became a mantra that pounded away inside my head.

Findcharliefindcharliefindcharliefindcharlie…

But my feet were glued to the tiled floor underneath them and I found that I couldn't just walk away without knowing for sure. If this couple were being completely truthful, and not practicing for some strange cosplay, then someone was definitely standing on the wrong continent. Even though I was absolutely certain that I wouldn't like the answer, I went ahead and turned back around.

"Pardon me, but did you say you were going to London tomorrow?"

"Aye, lad," he replied cheerfully. "I was stationed there during the war, then in Paris after we ran the Jerrys out of there. Annie's never been to London and I wanted to show her some of the places I'd been, maybe squeeze in some visits to the libraries that are still standing, I was an archivist before the war in Edinburgh, and then it's off across the channel for us next."

Oh hell… I thought to myself as I realized with a sinking feeling in my gut that they were not acting at all. What that meant for me as far as alternative explanations were concerned, wasn't looking too good.

"So were you posted over here too?" Annie asked me. And, with no clue on even where to begin explaining my presence in their reality, I simply lied through my teeth.

"Ah, no," I said after a frantic pause. "Old college injury got me. Wound up getting stuck stateside and missed the whole thing I'm afraid."

"Pity," Sean replied. "Say, you wouldn't know how much farther it is to London from here, do you, lad? I still can't figure how I got lost between Portsmouth and London. I must have driven that route hundreds of times in the last two years alone."

I didn't answer and it was fortunate for me that it really wasn't that much of an effort on my part to have a dumbfounded look on my face that could be misread as a simple 'I don't know' by the couple.

“They probably had to re-route some of the roads especially with all the bombing, Sean,” Annie broke in, unknowingly coming to my rescue before Sean asked me the next question: Where, precisely, were we at? “We were just very lucky we came across the hotel when we did. I was afraid we would have to sleep in the car tonight.”

“Yeah, lucky,” I said then bit my tongue to keep from commenting how they might have been better off in the car. Then I was struck with a thought and the question just naturally followed.

“So, what do you guys think of this place? It’s really something, isn’t it? Especially that front entrance.”

“Oh my, yes,” Annie answered enthusiastically. “I don’t know how they got all that marble in place so soon after the war. And there is so much of it inside and out.”

“The woodwork with the gold inlay throughout the front lobby is pretty impressive work,” Sean chimed in. “They have an impressive little library even and the staff is pretty friendly too. Especially the young woman at the front desk, pretty little thing. What was her name again, Annie?”

“Liz, dear. But those uniforms the women wear here. They have the poor dears dressed up like men in jackets and slacks.”

"Well, they can't have them running about in swimwear, can they?" Sean retorted, then gave me a sly wink.

"Hardly," I replied with a very weak effort at a chuckle, "Well, I've kept you two from your dessert. Have a safe trip to London tomorrow."

"Lad, we can give you a lift to London, if that's where you're going," Sean called after me as I walked away. "Least we can do for a Yank after your lot helped up beat off the Jerrys."

"Thanks anyway, but I'm not heading for London."

"Well, where are you heading?"

"Right now," I said with a sigh. "I honestly haven't the slightest idea."

I'm pretty sure the looks they gave me as I walked off were something to behold, but quite frankly I had more important things to worry about right now. I'd managed to walk myself back from the edge of a breakdown only to jump headlong into complete insanity. Because insanity was the only logical explanation for me having a conversation with two people who truly believed that they were only a two or three-hour drive from post-war 1940s London, England. And to find those two lost souls in the very same hotel with another couple that believed they were only a short journey to a destination thousands of miles and on another continent away from a man who knew he was some five thousand miles from either of those couples, who knew he should only be a few hours' drive from twenty-first century Phoenix, Arizona. And the alternative was utterly impossible to believe. Wasn't it?

Suddenly, *find Charlie* had become *find Charlie now. Now, now, NOW!!!!!*

I wandered back into the casino and this time took a closer look at those hundreds of people milling about. The case for insanity suddenly looked like as open and shut as you would ever find. As I passed rows of slot machines, I saw a Native American, replete with buckskin tunic and pants and moccasin footwear. Behind him, a dark-skinned woman dressed in attire from Ancient Egypt. The next row over, an elderly Asian man in a kimono, a German woman who might have been attending Oktoberfest by the looks of her garments and a man dressed as if prepared for a Siberian winter.

Everywhere I looked I saw people from all the cultures and countries that I'd ever heard or read about—and even a few I had never heard of before—and I knew even without asking them that their individual stories would be similar to that of Sean and Annie's back in the restaurant as well as that Japanese couple I'd met, but not gotten the names of, during my first visit in the casino.

And, it appeared, to that of mine and Charlie's as well. We'd lost our way and had somehow found ourselves in this place. To my growing horror, of all of the people I encountered it truly seemed that only I was aware of just how lost we all really were.

I kept my feet moving and passed out of the slots area. As I made my way through I noticed that the casino was segregated by game types. Dice games here, roulette wheels over there. Wandering back into the area where all of the card tables were set up, I found a group of four tables loaded with folks playing No Limit Hold'em Poker. Had I not recently gone insane I might have been tempted to take up the one empty seat I located; this was my game and I played it ruthlessly. Every Thursday night at my place back in Colorado was poker night with five players who never realized they were merely my personal ATM machines for the evening.

My game. But not Charlie's.

Charlie played blackjack exclusively. I hated the game because I always suspected that the people who were very good at it were merely very good at counting cards. There was no true skill in that, aside from being blessed with a good memory. Not like poker. Poker required a player to not only play the cards, but the players behind them as well if one wanted to be good at the game.

But Charlie, he swore by blackjack and if he was anywhere inside this casino, then he had to be near wherever they were dealing blackjack.

I quickly flagged down one of the casino workers—I swear to you that it seemed to be a requirement for employment at this hotel that the women all had to look like they'd just stepped off the photoshoot for the latest Sports Illustrated Swimsuit issue—and the platinum blond pixie cut, who would make any man quickly forget the throaty beauty in the café, whose name I didn't bother to read smiled and pointed in the direction of the blackjack tables.

I hurried over, hoping to find Charlie, and grab onto the one lifeline I could count on to help drag me back from the edge and make some sense out of whatever the hell was going on. It wasn't hard to find him at all once I got to the area; his booming laugh at some joke he'd just heard was a welcoming beacon to my ears.

When I got to his table, the first thing I noticed was a ridiculous number of chips piled up around his area of the table. Much like I had seen at the baccarat table earlier, it looked like everyone at the table was doing well but Charlie's stack was approaching Mount Olympus in size. He was good at this game, I easily admit, but not *that* good. No one was.

The second thing I noticed was the enchanting young Carrie—still in her hotel uniform but her nametag was now gone—draped on Charlie's right arm and looking like she was there to stay. That wasn't the least bit ridiculous at all. He was good at that too, as I've mentioned before, and he really was *that* good in that arena.

"Hey, Pete," he exclaimed when he saw me. "Pull up a chair and join us."

"Not right now thanks," I said. "Hey, I think they got our bags mixed up and one of mine is in your room. I was hoping you could let me in so I could get it."

That seemed to me to be a perfectly reasonable explanation to get Charlie out of the casino where I could talk to him without any unwanted eavesdroppers. Unfortunately, my lifeline went and threw me the anchor and sank my plan in less than a heartbeat.

"No problem, buddy, here's the key." He flipped his room card in my direction with one of those Friday night goofy grins of his face that I knew all too well. "Just leave it in my room. I don't think I'll be needing it."

Somehow, Carrie managed to snuggle even closer to Charlie than she had before. Even as I snagged the tumbling card out of the air, I tried to come up with some excuse, some pretense to get Charlie up and moving. But something in both of their expressions told me that it wouldn't matter one bit what I said or did next. Charlie wasn't moving from that chair anytime soon and when he did, he wasn't doing it just to go off somewhere with me.

I'd lost my wingman, my lifeline and maybe my only hope of figuring out what had happened to us. Charlie turned back to the table, and his new girlfriend, without so much as another word in my direction and I stumbled away without any direction in mind other than to get away from the creature who'd once been my best friend.

Before I realized it, I found myself in an abandoned area of the casino, empty chairs stacked around a few unused card tables and standing face to face with Liz. How long she had been watching me, how much she had seen, I simply did not know. But there she stood with an odd, sad look in her eyes.

"Aren't you going to ask me how you can be of service?" And I am sure there was more than a hint of bitterness in my voice, certainly more than she deserved to be on the receiving end of.

"No," she replied without reproach for my tone. "At this moment, Mr. Childress, you are looking for any exit that will lead you back to the outside world. I simply can't help you with that. All I can suggest to you is this—perhaps you are looking for the way out of here in the wrong direction."

"What does that mean?" I asked in confusion.

Something from behind me suddenly caught her attention at that moment. Her eyes quickly flickered to whatever it was for a brief moment before returning to meet mine.

"Your room opens up to the central park," she said after a moment's pause. "We see so very few of our guests ever bother to go out and fully explore it. Perhaps you should visit it. You may find it to be peaceful and relaxing."

She moved suddenly then, as if to walk past me without another word. But just as she drew even with me, her lips just inches from my right ear, I heard her whisper in a tone almost too soft for me to hear.

"You might even find it very enlightening, Mr. Childress."

Then she was gone, moving on into the casino to engage some of the other guests in conversation. As I turned to watch her walk away, I noticed what it was that had distracted her earlier, what had appeared to make her suddenly cautious not only in what she said but how she appeared while saying it.

Standing out there in the middle of the casino, clearly scanning the crowd for someone in particular, was the hotel's manager. But before he could look over in my direction and take notice of me, I darted toward a much darker area of the casino and eventually made my way back around to the entrance without him seeing me at all. For a reason that I could not put a logical explanation to, I suddenly had a very strong urge to be as far away from that man as I could possibly get myself and do it as quickly as I could.

Even within the seemingly limited, but very gilded, confines of this nightmarish trap that I found myself in.

#

EIGHT

In all of the time he had been running this operation, he had never before run into this problem. This newfound discovery both vexed him and gave him yet another small reason to hope, all at the same time.

He had lost track of a guest.

The manager, using his ever-present pad, could track anyone within the hotel to within a foot of their actual location on demand. But, after entering the casino for the second time, Peter Childress disappeared, at least as far as the pad's tracking was concerned. Surprised, the manager had stared dumbly at the screen for a full thirty seconds before moving toward the casino entrance in long, quick strides.

He did not think Childress had found a way out, but he wanted to get a visual on him just to make sure. As he worked his way through the vast gaming area, the object of his search continued to elude him. Even a quick reboot of the pad failed to offer any clue as to where Childress had gotten off to.

Just as he was about to abandon his search, the manager spotted Liz making her way toward the employee's entrance located in the rear of the casino. He watched her all the way across the room, wondering exactly why she would have been in the casino to begin with. It wasn't her regular area of operation. The thought that she might be in here to meet with Childress died the instant she opened the door and departed the room.

At almost the same moment, the pad in his hand bleeped softly for his attention. Looking down, his eyes widened as he saw that Childress was once again showing on the tracker and that he was walking away from the main entrance to the casino and heading toward the elevators.

His heart skipped a beat as he considered exactly what Childress' vanishing and reappearing act meant. This had never happened before and it clearly wasn't a glitch in the system. He needed to figure out how and why it had happened to Childress and he could not do that while standing here.

He made his way back through the crowded room and headed back to his office as quickly as he could without alarming any of the guests or staff. Locking the door behind him, the manager crossed the spartanly decorated office. A simple dark wood desk, with a matching dark wood filing cabinet and a single chair accounted for all of the furniture in the room. The only décor in the room was a wall-sized painting—an ocean scene at night with a full moon rising just above the horizon.

The manager walked straight to the painting and reached up to lay his open palm on the largest crater of the moon. With a slight *snicking* sound from behind the painting, the entire wall silently swung open, revealing a panel of monitors and a single keyboard. Laying his hand on top of a clear plate next to the keyboard, he waited as a scanner quickly swept up and down, bathing his open palm in bright white light. When it had completed its pass, the panel flared to life. Most of the monitors displayed the common areas of the hotel while the primary monitor located just above the keyboard rotated through a steady stream of reports and updates. The reports went unnoticed as the manager focused his attention on the monitor dedicated to the casino.

"Call up the casino," he said aloud, seemingly addressing the air. "Starting with the time of arrival of Mr.

Childress inside and continue playback on up until his departure."

"Working," replied a disembodied voice, even though no obvious speaker could be seen anywhere on the panel. "Ready."

"Run."

The monitor flickered from a live shot of the casino to a quad screen showing four different angles of the casino. The manager could see Childress enter the casino, leave for the café and then return. He followed Childress' progress through the different game areas until he encountered his friend. After their conversation, Childress walked away and wandered into a darkened area of the room where he encountered Liz.

But no matter how he tried to adjust the view, he could not get a good enough look at the pair to make out what it was they said. At length, the two parted company and Childress exited. It was at this point when the manager's pad had picked the man back up. Frustrated that he had been unable to glean any useful information, the manager stepped away from the panel and reached to swing the wall back into place. He would have to resume his careful watch on Mr. Childress and see what developed.

But even as his hand closed on the wall's edge, he was struck by a thought. Perhaps Mr. Childress wasn't the one in need of closer observation.

Liz.

* * * * *

Liz was uncertain if she had escaped the casino unseen by the manager. His ability to seemingly appear out of thin air at the most inconvenient times was somewhat frightening, especially at this particular point in time.

She had hoped the confusion of the large crowd would give her an opportunity to speak alone and at length with Childress. Knowing that he would almost certainly go to his friend at some point for aid, she had kept as near as she could to Womack while keeping an eye out for Childress.

She could tell that the conversation with Womack hadn't gone the way he had hoped it would. Luck was on her side when he walked away from the blackjack table and headed directly in her direction. She drew back a little further into the abandoned area and waited until Childress arrived before speaking with him.

There hadn't been as much time as she had hoped for before she had spotted the manager nearby. All she could hope for was that she had planted the seed in his mind and that he would go where she desperately needed him to go next. Having taken up the station behind the desk, she watched, without seeming to be doing so, Childress headed for the elevators. She could only assume he would use them to return to his room.

As for what he would do next, she could only watch the monitor, track his movements through his key card, hope for the best and pray that her never-ending nightmare was close to its conclusion.

NINE

The pair of men dressed in Roman togas that greeted me cordially in the elevator hardly made an impression on me by this point. I stepped in, called out my room number and leaned up against the far wall, as far away from the men as I could get in the enclosed space.

From where I stood, I could clearly see the lips moving and the words being formed there were clearly in ancient Latin—I took a year of the language to fill out the credits on my first degree—but I heard every word spoken in very modern English.

"I tell you, Justus," the older-looking man of the pair said, resuming the conversation my arrival had interrupted. "There simply is no possibility of completing construction in the allotted time. This concrete they are raving about in Cosa may be everything they are saying about it. But it still takes time to mix it, pour it and allow it to set no matter how loudly Senator Albanus raises his voice at me."

"Like the majority of the Senate, Decimus," the younger man replied dryly, "Albanus cares little for the reasons as to why the world does not simply leap at his every command, he simply demands that it do so anyway."

"Perhaps Albanus and the Senate should focus more on their attention to defeating Pyrrhus," Decimus responded with a huff. "Perhaps they should get that done before Carthage decides to take Sicily once and for all. And you know all too well, where they will cast their eyes next."

"Surely," Justus scoffed lightly. "You aren't lending any credence to that ridiculous prediction of Pyrrhus, are you? Carthage wouldn't dare go to war with Rome over that miserable excuse of an island."

"I do indeed," Decimus replied. "And it is likely to happen long before I can complete construction on the new Hall of Justice, especially if those know-it-all Senators keep meddling with my design. I have raised buildings all over the Republic for longer than most of them have been alive. You would think they might allow that I know what I am doing by now."

"Decimus, my old mentor," Justus replied with a chuckle. "The day that happens will be the day I have more gray hairs on my head than you do now on yours."

The older man joined in on the laugh as the doors parted and the men exited the cab. I didn't bother to ask them what they had seen upon their arrival here, I had a pretty good idea it would match the construction and design style of an Old Roman Insula—a type of glorified apartment complex—that I had studied a long time ago back in school. Besides, I had more important matters to consider than the conversation of two men who should have died over two thousand years before I had been born. Like why I would see such a conversation and automatically assume I was still sane, for starters.

The doors closed and the elevator moved up to the next level, mine, and when the doors opened once again, I stepped out and started down the corridor. But before I could reach the relative safety of my room, even if such a term applied anywhere within these walls, the hotel had one more surprise to spring on me.

An Egyptian couple, right off the hieroglyphs from an ancient pyramid tomb, stepped out into the hallway from a nearby room. The man wore a basic white linen tunic and skirt with a belt of gold and the woman wore a full-length dress of blue linen lined with horizontally zig-zagging rows of white and a gold headband with what looked like a ruby, held in place by a pair of bird-like creatures, in the center.

I stopped dead in my tracks and just stared as they approached. I can only imagine the look on my face. By now, it was probably permanently etched in place.

"Are you unwell, my friend?" the man asked, placing a hand on my arm just below the shoulder as if to keep me from keeling over on my face. Which, come to think of it, was starting to sound like a pretty good idea right about now. Like the Romans in the elevator, the movement of his lips did not match the English words I heard.

"Just a bit of a headache," I lied in reply. "It has been a long day."

"My husband, Ammon, is a healer in Memphis," the woman said, and somehow I knew without a doubt that she did not mean the city in Tennessee either. "He can help you."

"Ah yes," Ammon said. "I can boil down some willow bark. It will take away your pain."

Of that I had no doubt, because we call the product of that recipe aspirin where I come from. *Where or when?* I found myself wondering suddenly as the thought occurred that the Memphis in Egypt, the one I knew the woman had mentioned, no longer existed and hadn't for a very long time. I must have turned another shade of pale at that moment, for Ammon suddenly lunged forward and grabbed me by both arms.

"Come, my friend, you are not well at all," he exclaimed. "Nenet, help me with him."

I allowed the couple to escort me down the hall until we reached my room. After assuring them that I would be just fine as soon as I lay down and rested, and thanking them for their concern, I quickly stepped through the doorway and closed the door on the growing insanity beyond it.

It had taken me a couple of swipes to get the door opened in the first place before I realized the reason why the door wasn't opening. I still had Charlie's room card in my hand. After swapping cards and getting into the room, I tossed both cards onto the top of the desk.

I sat down heavily on the bed, giving momentary thought to lying down and closing my eyes for a minute. But my brain raced too much for that. Putting aside the improbability of just about every aspect of what I had discovered of this strange place, including that momentary thought of having somehow travelled in time, I tried to focus my attention on the primary problem while fighting down the fear that I was losing my mind. It was clear, no matter what was happening to me, that finding some type of exit that would lead me back to the outside world where everything made sense was my only hope.

Losing Charlie to this place was a terrible blow. It was as if my own right arm had been ripped away. Until this very moment, I had never truly realized how much I valued and even depended on having him as a colleague and as a friend. No project had seemed too overwhelming, no obstacle too imposing to overcome whenever it was the two of us together tackling it.

But without him, now I found that I was completely at a loss at what I should do next. Should I confront the manager, risking that whoever was responsible for this place would then become aware that whatever it was that made the others blindly accept this charade had not worked its magic on me? Should I spend countless more hours, even days perhaps, wandering a place that seemed to stretch on to infinity—at least on the inside—looking for some passageway to the outside, assuming of course that there even was one?

Lost in thought, I just sat there and stared blankly out the window and at the interior park that lay beyond. It was the park that the enigmatic desk clerk, Liz, had just made a very strong point of mentioning to me downstairs in the casino. It was damned difficult to get a solid read on the woman—and trust me that is a very difficult admission for a poker player like me to make—and I could at least partly blame it on the situation I found myself in. When one's sanity was under question, it then became very difficult to really know with any absolute certainty what was up, down, left or right any longer.

At times, it seemed to me that she was trying to dropping hints, almost trying to warn me of trouble. But at other times, she seemed to be just as much a major part of the overall wrongness of the place as anything else in here was, short of the manager himself of course. If she really had been trying to hint at trouble, then why had she not just come out and told us so as soon as we walked in the door, when we might have been able to turn right back around and get back outside?

But in fairness, I wondered, had it already been too late at that point? Had the two of us been damned the instant we crossed the threshold, like Renfield had when he'd willingly walked into Dracula's castle? I racked my memory of our checking in, trying to recall if I had ever looked back behind us. Had I seen the doors at any point after we entered and reached the desk? I simply did not recall, not even after I had entered the elevator and turned back to face the lobby when I should have seen them if but briefly.

Or had it been someone else's presence nearby instead that had prevented her from doing anything for us? The manager had been there in the lobby when we checked in, I had briefly seen him standing on the walkway above later, and once again in the casino. It had been his arrival that had suddenly cut short my conversation with Liz in the casino minutes ago. Was she so afraid of him that she feared being seen speaking with me for more than just a short period of time, as if she was just an employee helping out a guest, or was there some other reason for her not wanting him to be privy to our meeting?

There was an avalanche of questions rumbling through my brain but no answers to be found anywhere. The headache that I had only slightly lied to Ammon about out in the hall decided to make its presence known. So I got off the bed, hoping some fresh air would help, and walked to the rear door. I opened the door, leaving it open behind me as I took a couple of steps out onto the grass and took another look around.

Looking in the wrong direction.

That was the gist of what she had said to me just before she had made a point of mentioning this very park.

But what was the purpose of her doing so? Was the way out of this nightmare really waiting for me to find somewhere out there? Or was there a more sinister purpose behind her suggestion? I just stood there staring at the foliage until I finally decided that just sitting in my room wouldn't get anything done so I might as well go on out there and see whatever it was that I could find.

The grass beneath my feet was real enough and the natural give from the ground as I stepped along meant there was also very real earth lying underneath the grass. This wasn't an artificial surface of shredded tires painted green like the turf laid down in an indoor football stadium. Figuring that the doors to the neighboring rooms would be of little use to my search, provided they were even unlocked and accessible, I kept walking straight ahead.

The size of the area struck me again. No matter how far I walked, I still could not see the other side of the park where there surely had to be another wall of the tower. The only other human being I encountered on my journey was one of the hotel employees, his nametag identified him as Noah. He whistled a tune I didn't recognize, trimming a row of bushes when he spotted me.

"G'day, mate," Noah greeted me with a light Aussie accent. "You're a bit off the beaten path."

And better still. Between the blue grass and the water was a solid white wall with an old wooden door.

It was weathered and worn, the hinges were rusty and the doorknob's black paint was faded and chipped and it was the best damn looking door I'd ever seen in my entire life. I practically ran around the edge of the lake until I reached the opening in the trees and then dashed up to the door, caressing it like a long-lost lover. I had found the way out. I was absolutely certain of that. I reached for the knob, grasped it and started to turn it to open the door.

And then all hell broke loose.

The blue grass that had covered the mound of what I had thought to be dirt began to move. Higher and higher it went until it formed a bipedal creature no less than a dozen feet tall. It looked every bit like an enormous blue-furred teddy bear. Only this "teddy bear" had glowing, angry red eyes and a snarling mouth full of razor sharp teeth. It looked down at me as if it had just discovered that lunch had been delivered and it was very, very hungry.

"Oh, shit!" I exclaimed.

I stood there, frozen in place, and just gaped at the monstrosity. That is, I stood there until the thing clubbed me with a not-so-soft paw, razor sharp claws and all. A surprisingly pleasant feeling of flying through the air was quickly followed by the not-so-pleasant feeling of landing, very hard, on top of one of the unyielding mounds of earth. The grass covering them did nothing at all to cushion my impact. Rolling to a stop on the other side, the pain from the impact got around to announcing itself to my brain. But before I even had a chance to inspect the damaged area, I got backhanded—or back pawed if you will—into flight again.

I didn't even have time to finish wondering how the big lummox had managed to cover all that ground that quickly before my flight came to an abrupt end. This time the landing involved a couple of bushes that did a much better job of cushioning the blow but also did a very good job of adding to the damage the homicidal teddy bear had already inflicted on me. This time when I rolled to a halt against one of the small trees, I didn't bother to take inventory of the damage. I just pulled myself up with the aid of a perfectly placed branch of the tree I'd rolled into and ran away as fast as I could under the circumstances.

Following the brook as best I could, that is with a blood-thirsty behemoth hot on my trail, I stayed as close as I could to every tree, bush or obstacle that I could find along the way to try to slow down my hefty pursuer. I could hear its huffing growl behind me. I swear I even felt it breathing down my neck more than once along the way, as it smashed its way through the foliage. I cannot describe the relief I felt when I finally spotted the trees that I had used as a marker. Once I reached them, I turned left and dashed over the hill.

The sight of the open door to my room was one of the most beautiful I'd ever seen in my life. The open door not only marked which in the row of doors was the one that led to my own room, it also meant that I'd be able to get into my room without any problems or delay. For I had stupidly left my room card inside on the desk before I'd come out here in the park. Frantic and all but certain that another blow would land on me before I could reach the door, I sped across the open area as fast as my legs could carry me.

When I got near enough, I hurled myself into the opening. But I had badly misjudged the distance and I wound up slamming hard into the foot of the bed. With every square inch of my body screaming in pain, I somehow managed to hook a foot on the door and slammed it shut. Rolling over, I grabbed onto the desk and hauled it in front of the door. Bracing my back against the desk, I planted both feet against the bed and waited for the inevitable smash of an enraged fifteen-foot-tall, electric-blue teddy bear slamming into the door at full speed.

I waited. I waited and I waited some more.

After what seemed like a very long time, I opened my eyes.

"It's safe. He's not out there any longer. Everything is fine now."

Liz was seated in the large chair stationed between the head of the bed and the bathroom door. Calm and collected, legs chastely crossed, she'd obviously been sitting there for quite some time. Long enough, at any rate, to have seen my mad dash for safety and remain seated like there wasn't a thing wrong in the world.

I got up slowly and looked outside for myself. Sure enough that big blue menace wasn't anywhere to be seen. Nor could I find any trace of the path of destruction it must have caused going through that last set of trees. It was almost as if the entire incident had never happened, except of course for my many injuries.

But when I looked down at my arms and torso, where claw marks and sharp branches had cut me up pretty good, I saw the wounds starting to close, healing so completely that within moments, there wasn't even so much as a scar or any other type of mark to indicate they'd ever been there in the first place. Then the torn clothing began to mend itself as well, leaving not so much as a wrinkle behind when whatever was happening had completed its work.

Even the pain associated with the injuries had faded until not even the memory of the pain remained. Numb, I stared at my arms as if they were something alien to me. When I turned to look at Liz, she had the strangest expression of pity, sadness and relief on her face that I had ever seen before.

"What in hell is this place?" I asked in a hoarse whisper. At my inquiry, a tear escaped her left eye and quickly streaked down her face.

"Funny that you should put it quite that way," she replied, her voice only slightly less shaky than mine had been. "What do you know of Purgatory?"

More than I'd care to admit to be honest. I'd been raised in a Catholic family but I had quickly drifted away from the Church very soon after graduating from high school. I had never been one for blind faith and there were just a few too many things in Catholicism that required that kind of faith for my taste.

My separation from the Church had begun the day I had questioned our bishop on the whole concept of the

Holy Trinity. God sent himself down to Earth and, after praying to himself, allowed mankind to kill him. Then, after three days of being dead, He raised Himself up from the grave? It didn't work for me. Had I stayed in the Church, I had little doubt I was on track to be ex-communicated before my twenty-fifth birthday. They might have even brought back branding someone as a heretic solely on my account alone.

Even as a very young child, I'd had an issue with the concept that a loving creator of life would also be so cruel as to send his creations to such a terrible place as Hell for eternity. Nor could I accept that same creator to have a place of punishment where a soul found itself on the precipice with ascension to Heaven or being cast into Hellfire in the balance.

A slight doubt suddenly tickled the back of my brain. Maybe the old bishop had been right after all. But there was just one slight detail that chased away the newfound doubt.

"I don't remember dying," I said aloud to Liz. "I'm pretty sure you have to do that first before winding up there. Do you remember dying?"

"No," she said, brushing away her tears. "No I don't. But how else do you explain this place?"

"I can't. But I only just got here so I don't know a whole lot about it. At least, not as much as someone who has apparently been around here a lot longer than I have."

A strange flicker of emotion crossed her face but she remained silent, almost as if she were afraid of the next question. *How long have you been here?* Tell you the truth, I was a little afraid of the answer myself. Because I was starting to realize how much activity there had been since arriving here and yet I had no sense of any significant passage of time. I decided to save the question for a little later.

"Okay. I know for a fact that the stainless steel wall across from the front desk had been a glass entryway when Charlie and I walked into this hotel."

"That is true, for you and your friend."

"What do you mean, for us?"

"The hotel's exterior and interior appears differently to everyone," she answered. "With the only exception being for those who have entered it at the same time."

"You mean it keeps changing?"

"No, it's not so much that it changes. It's just that it is being perceived differently by each of us. For example, this chair I am sitting in. The chair I see is a Wainscot

Chair made of oak with a paisley cushion on the seat. Is that the description of the chair that you see me sitting in?"

I shook my head. It wasn't. It wasn't even close.

"You're sitting in a heavily padded armchair," I said softly. "All covered in some type of gray material. Not even so much as a sliver of wood in sight."

We went around the entire room that way and it was more of the same. The geography of the room was the same, the window and doors were in the same place of course. But the architectural style and décor were nearly polar opposites. They were separated by decades at least, if not even a century or two.

"Is it like this throughout the entire hotel?" I asked, my mind struggling to wrap itself around what I was being told.

"It seems to vary in degrees from room to room but as far as I can tell, yes."

"So no one notices anything amiss with the rooms. But what about the clothes? I've seen people dressed in some pretty wild stuff. No one else has noticed?"

"No, as far as I can tell it is just you and me. Everyone else sees the other guests and hotel employees attired in the same fashion style that they are expecting to see."

Look, I'm sorry but I'm a guy and we are notorious for thinking sometimes without using the brain. I started out wondering if, by expecting her to be wearing something else, that I would see the material as it changed styles. Which was quickly followed up with the thought, *or wearing nothing at all.* Fortunately for me, her outfit did not change at all. But the corner of her mouth twitched slightly as she noticed where I was looking so intently.

"I'm still wearing the same yellow dress I had on the very first day when I came here," she said. "What do you see?"

"It looks really good on you," I added after I'd described what passed for the hotel uniform from my perspective. She flashed a quick smile, obviously pleased by the compliment, and I had a feeling she had read me like an open book just a few moments ago. The blush that I'm sure was on my face was probably a dead giveaway. So much for my famed poker face, at least when in a place like this it seemed. But she wasn't saying anything more about it right now, to my relief, and that made a lot of sense. We had some more pressing issues to deal with right now.

"So when a new guest arrives to check in, do they just appear to walk through what looks like to you a solid wall?"

"No. I never see a new arrival until they are near the front desk. One instant, the area is clear of any activity and the next there is someone, sometimes more than one at that, walking toward me out of thin air. It takes some getting used to."

"I can just bet. So they check in and enjoy the amenities and never realize at all how much time has actually passed?"

"No, they don't," she replied sadly. "Some stay here as guests. Others go to work for the hotel, like I did. But for the guests, tomorrow's check-out time is always tomorrow and for the staff, the end of the shift never comes. Time just doesn't seem to exist in here as we know it. Unfortunately, we're just the only ones who seem to notice that."

"Has anyone ever gotten out of this place?" I asked as I sat down on the bed.

"Not that I am aware of since I arrived," she replied. "I have no idea what transpired before then."

"Has anyone ever really tried?"

"There were a couple of people, obviously I don't actually know how long ago it was," she began. "The first was a young woman named Jocelyn. Right from the first, I could see that she didn't believe a single thing she saw. Then, one day she came to me and told me about a door she'd found on the far side of the park. She hadn't tried to open it and didn't even try to draw near to it. She said it felt like the door wanted her to go away, so she did. After that, I hardly ever saw her around and she never mentioned the door again. As far as I can tell, she is still a guest here.

"Then there was a man from France, Jean-Claude, that I thought was my best chance to help me escape. He was a lot like you. He instantly knew something wasn't quite right but couldn't put his finger on it. So one day I told him about the door and that I thought it was the way out of here. So we went out to find it."

"What happened?" I asked.

"As soon as he touched the door, that monster arose and attacked us. We were lucky to escape. But after that, Jean-Claude never spoke another word to me. I've only seen him once since and he looks like he has become like the others. For all I…."

"Now wait just a damned minute," I interrupted hotly, jumping up to my feet to glower down at her. "You *knew* about that monster out there before you all but led me out to that door? What in the hell were you trying to do, get me killed?!"

"Would you have believed me if I had told you everything?" she replied calmly, with yet a haunted look in her eyes. “Would you have believed anything you’ve seen or that I’ve told you since if you hadn’t seen it all for yourself?”

I opened my mouth to say that I sure as hell would have and then just as quickly shut it. Because she was absolutely right. Until I’d seen and felt it myself, as improbable as the entire experience had been, I would not have believed her for even a single second.

“Okay,” I said as I sat back down. “I’m sorry. You’ve got a point there. I probably wouldn’t have believed you at that. So exactly what is it about the two of us that allows us to know something’s isn’t right here while everyone else in here has no clue they are stuck in neutral?”

“I don’t know Peter and I don’t know how would we figure it out.”

“Maybe it is in the way we came to be here,” I said, musing aloud. “Why don’t you tell me how you wound up here in the first place and I’ll see if anything matches with what happened to Charlie and me.”

“That sounds like as good as any starting place,” she said. “Then maybe you can answer a question for me?”

“I can try. What’s the question?”

“After I finish telling you how I arrived at the Infinity, I will tell you what year it was. Then you can tell me what was the year when you came here and then I'll know how long I've been trapped here."

There was something about the emphasis she put on the word year, both times for that matter, that told me she knew that quite some time had passed between our respective arrivals here. Suddenly, as she began to tell me her story, I found that I was filled with dread at what the answer to her question would mean.

For the both of us.

TEN

Life in mid-nineteenth century LaGrange, Georgia—a community located less than a dozen miles east of the Alabama state line—for a young girl born to a family not overly wealthy but still financially prominent in the community, was as near to heavenly perfection as anyone would hope to find anywhere else on Earth.

Elizabeth Ann Wright was the only child born to Nathan and Juliana Smithfield Wright. Their child had arrived so late in their life that Juliana had all but given up any hope of her ever experiencing motherhood. So when Elizabeth, or Lizzie as her parents both quickly took to calling her, was born on a warm spring day, there was a great celebration within the entire household as well as the rest of the city of LaGrange.

Nathan Wright was the town's mayor at the time of his daughter's arrival and he was also the owner of the lumber mill. He had taken his oversight of his growing town just as seriously as he did growing his business, and both entities had prospered under his attentions. But those responsibilities did not preclude him from devoting just as much of his time and energy on his family. And while the family may not have further multiplied, it had prospered quite well.

A stern Southern gentleman of the old order, Nathan was considered something of a progressive in the manner in which he treated the people who worked for him, at his house, at his business and in general. He owned no slaves, never had and would never consider owning one. Nor was he the type of man that wanted a house filled with empty-headed women.

His wife Juliana was a trusted advisor in many of his business affairs. While Juliana went about seeing to it that their daughter lacked nothing of the social graces expected of a young Southern girl, Nathan saw to it that his daughter would be able to use her brain for something, as he often put it to the girl herself, other than pretty-looking shoulder ballast.

Miss Elizabeth had inherited her father's love of reading and eagerly took to the challenge of helping him with the various ledgers from his business and household accounts. The year before her debutante ball, she was officially on the payroll as his company's bookkeeper.

When the Wright's house was decked out in all of its grand finery for her ball, it was remarked by all in attendance that she was certainly one of the most self-possessed seventeen-year-old ladies anyone could ever recall having ever resided in the entire county, if not the state of Georgia itself. And none among the attendees that evening, especially the eligible young men, would dare argue against her being one of the prettiest as well.

And she certainly was a vision that night in a dress that appeared to have been spun from pure gold. Every single eligible bachelor within riding distance was present that evening, all vying for just a moment of her slightest attention. But Nathan had raised his daughter too well in every aspect of life to fall for just any stranger—no matter how tall, dark or handsome he might have been—and in fact, she already had her sights squarely set on the young man she had decided to spend the rest of her life with.

William Caldwell had arrived in LaGrange just the year before, after graduating from college in Atlanta. Orphaned at a very young age and raised by a stern but kindly widower uncle, William had worked hard for his uncle's railroad as he grew older. But his uncle also worked his nephew's brain equally as hard as he had his muscles, wanting his sister's only child to become something more than just another railroad man in his company.

So he sent William to the best school to be found in all of Georgia, where the young man had quickly discovered a great love of the law and his desire to become a lawyer. And because William was also skilled with his hands, he took a job at Wright's lumber mill to help supplement his income while he established his new practice. He had laid the foundation for his future in the same town where he had discovered the woman he wanted to spend the rest of his life with.

Nathan had been quite taken himself with young William, treating him almost as if he was the son that he'd never been blessed with. Nathan fully approved of William's courtship of his only child. Not long after William had arrived in LaGrange, showing himself to be a hardworking man, he had begun practicing law. Nathan had proudly walked Elizabeth down the aisle and placed her hand in William's.

In just two short years, both Nathan and William had seen increasing success in their respective business ventures just as the young couple welcomed their own daughter, Audie, to the world. Nathan had lived just long enough to hear his granddaughter's very first words, falling down dead from a heart attack while walking home from his mill one evening.

"His heart just gave out," the old town doctor reported to the family with great sadness. He had helped deliver both Elizabeth and her daughter into the world. At the funeral service two days later, the entire town had turned out to say their final goodbyes to their beloved mayor.

Juliana quickly devoted herself to her granddaughter as much as anyone possibly could. But her whole life had been so entwined with that of Nathan's that it surprised no one at all when they'd gone into her room one morning only to discover that she had died peacefully in her sleep sometime during the night. Barely six months after Nathan had been laid to rest, Juliana joined him at his side in the LaGrange Cemetery.

LaGrange had suddenly become a much less bright place in Elizabeth's eyes, despite William's best efforts to help her through her grief at losing both parents so close together. Not too long after Audie's third birthday, William was certain that he had discovered a way to lift some of the weight of grief that rested heavily on his wife's heart.

Robert Malcolm Ferguson was considered the wealthiest man in Atlanta, and was rumored to be the richest in all of Georgia if not the entire South itself, and he had a plan to increase his holdings tenfold. Ferguson wanted to build up a shipping empire to end all shipping empires, from ships at sea, to wagon trains and even a multi-state rail system.

To attain his lofty goals, Ferguson employed only the best and brightest wherever he could find them. And he spared no expense looking for them. He had recalled an ambitious young nephew of a business associate, one with experience working with railroads, who was mentioned as an up-and-coming lawyer out in western Georgia. This young up and comer was clearly a perfect fit for his organization. So he sent a telegram off to William Caldwell, Esq. inviting him and his wife to come to Atlanta to discuss him joining Ferguson Shipping.

William had instantly known that it was an opportunity of a lifetime, and even though it would mean leaving LaGrange behind, Elizabeth's spirits seemed to pick up at the thought of moving to Atlanta. Mildred, a distant cousin on her mother's side, suggested that perhaps the two of them should make the three-day round trip and leave little Audie in her care in LaGrange.

"How often can the two of you get some time alone?" Mildred said. "Go on to the big city and have some fun. The two of us will be just fine."

Little Audie adored Mildred, who treated the child like a princess, and the young parents happily accepted the offer. And while Elizabeth dearly missed her child, she enjoyed every minute of their stay in Atlanta. Mrs. Ferguson had been a perfect hostess and assured Elizabeth that she would fit right into Atlanta society once her young family had moved up from LaGrange.

"I know Robert," the older woman said over tea. "He simply will not take no for an answer. You might as well have just packed up and brought everything up with you."

Mrs. Ferguson knew her husband well indeed, for the offer he had made to William was more than the young lawyer or Elizabeth could have ever dared dream for. The thought of turning the offer down was never a possibility either of them considered.

When they returned to LaGrange, tired from the journey, the excitement of the pending future hadn't been dulled in any way by the daunting task of making the move. But it had been exceeded by the couple's eagerness to see their daughter again.

Eagerness quickly turned to concern when they arrived home and could not find either Mildred or Audie anywhere. Their time of return had been known before they'd left for Atlanta and surely Mildred would have made sure that Audie was here to greet her parents. Thinking that perhaps she had taken the child to her home and had lost track of time, they had gone there to look for them.

But nothing but silence, as well as a lot of locked doors and windows, were all that greeted the worried parents' arrival there. Frantic inquiries with the nearest neighbors yielded little to no information as no one had seen them since the day before. Concern now became worry and near panic as the two parents turned to the town marshal for help.

"She probably took the child down to the creek," the marshal soothed. "I saw some huckleberries that looked pretty close to ripe for the picking just last week. We're liable to come upon them with a basket of berries each in hand."

Stepping out of his office, the marshal flagged down several of the townsmen to look around town for the missing pair beyond the city proper, while he and his lone deputy went over to Mildred's home to have a look around for themselves. The marshal forced the flimsy lock on the door and entered the home to find pretty much what he had expected in the home of a single woman who lived alone. Everything was neat, clean and tidy.

Right up until the moment he stepped into the lone bedroom in the house.

"Damn it to hell," the marshal swore softly at the scene before his eyes, knowing he would see it over and over every single time he closed his eyes until the day of his passing. "Roy, go on and fetch the doctor and tell him to get over here. After you've sent him on his way, you wait two minutes and then you go find the Caldwells. Tell them we found little Audie, nothing else you hear, and then you bring them here, but you don't let them come inside. I'll meet you all out front."

The deputy's view of the bedroom was fully blocked by the marshal, who gave no indication that he had any intention of moving out of the way any time soon. The deputy wanted to ask why he needed to wait for two minutes. He wanted to ask what else he should say when he found the Caldwells. He wanted to ask what the marshal had found in that room.

Then he took a closer look at the marshal's face and found all of the answers to his questions sitting there, just as he suspected the Caldwells would now find their answers on his face when he found them. Without another word, he turned around and left the home to find the doctor and left the marshal behind with his grim find.

Little Audie was laid out on the bed, hair neatly combed and in a fine dress, looking for all the world as if she were merely taking a nap and would wake up at any moment. The peaceful look on her face was heartbreaking. The marshal had seen his share of dead bodies before, enough to know one when he was looking right at it.

But in the way of the human race when faced with such a terrible tragedy, he moved toward the little girl and touched her pale cheek, hoping against all hope that he was wrong. She was cold, the depth of cold that only a dead human body seemed able to attain.

He needed no such confirming touch for Mildred, who lay in the bed next to Audie. The older woman held a straight razor in her left hand. She had used it to slit both of her wrists as she had lain next to Audie and had simply let all of her blood drain out.

Walking around the bed, the marshal picked up the note that Mildred had left on the nightstand beside her bed. It had been left on top of a clean white rag and propped up against a bottle. It was addressed to the Caldwells, but he was duty-bound to read it for himself.

She began with an apology for what she was about to do and followed with a brief explanation of why. Unmarried and well past her twentieth birthday, Mildred had given up hope of marriage and motherhood. By the end of the second day of having Audie with her, she had found that she could not bear the thought of giving her back and being alone once again once the Caldwells had moved to Atlanta. She had closed the letter by assuring her cousin that she would take good care of their precious Audie until that glorious day when Elizabeth and William joined them in heaven.

Nathan Wright had been a good friend of the marshal. That his granddaughter should have been murdered in the town that he was sworn to protect brought upon him such a sudden flash of rage that he wanted to grab the dead woman in both hands and… and… God only knew what he wanted to do.

But he could not do so because he was an officer of the law and would not do so because it would do no good to anyone any more than it would not bring back this lost child. With an effort, he checked his anger, though it would be some time before the warmth of his rage would burn out, and sat vigil over the little dead girl while he waited for the doctor.

Barely a minute had passed before he heard the outer door open and close and he listened to the footsteps as the doctor walked in. The deputy must have already warned him as to what awaited him in this room as there was no shock on his face, only a deep sadness as he looked at the bed.

"One of my greatest joys as a doctor," he said, voice heavy with emotion, "is when I help bring a new life into this world like I did the both of them. I don't know how many more of them I can bear to see depart it before I do. Oh, you poor dear children."

The doctor sat down on the bed next to Audie and, like the marshal had earlier, placed a hopeful hand against her cheek. A tear unashamedly rolled down his face at the final confirmation that there was nothing he could do.

"We know why she did it at least," the marshal said, holding out the note to the doctor to take. "And we know how."

The marshal picked up the bottle and the rag and showed it to the doctor. The label read chloroform.

"She came by my office yesterday, had little Audie with her," the doctor said, a pained look on his face. "She said she'd been feeling unwell and wanted to know if I had any smelling salts. She must have taken it while I was filling a small bottle of them for her to take home."

"It wasn't your fault, doctor," the marshal said as he watched the old man's face turn ashen. "If she hadn't gotten her hands on this bottle, she just would have found another way to do it. At least the child didn't suffer this way. Come along now, let's get her out of here."

The marshal moved back around the bed and started to lift little Audie up.

"Why?"

"I think it would be better if her parents didn't see her in here like this, don't you?"

"No. No, I wouldn't want them to see her in here," the doctor answered as he moved aside. "You take care of her, and them; leave me to deal with this."

The marshal nodded, the doctor was also the undertaker and county coroner. If he'd had just a little too much to drink at dinner, sometimes he'd joke that at least he got to bury his mistakes. The marshal knew that this burial would haunt the doctor, and him as well to a great extent, for quite some time. The marshal carried the girl outside to the front yard just as her parents arrived.

No words were said. None were needed. He gently handed the girl's lifeless body to her mother and stepped back. Elizabeth hugged her daughter's body close, her face a desolate mask of anguish and despair, her mouth opened and closed over and over but no sound came out as she sank to her knees onto the grass next to the steps.

Helpless to do anything else but watch, William stood next to his wife and the shock of the loss had already seemed to have aged him ten years since he'd arrived at the scene. It was his duty as her father to keep her safe and, through absolutely no fault of his own, he had utterly failed her. The marshal handed William the note so that he would know what he needed to know. He would know who had taken his daughter, why it had been done and that his daughter's killer would harm no one else, not ever again.

He would have the knowledge, the marshal knew from past experience, but he would never gain the understanding. Some might say that knowing helped. They were wrong.

"Take your wife and child on home, Will," the marshal said kindly, regaining possession of the suicide note. It would be needed for the coroner's inquest. "There's nothing more to be done here right now, son. See to your family."

William dully nodded and leaned down to help Elizabeth to her feet. That was the moment when she began shrieking. The only two words that came out of her mouth that any of those present could make out were Audie's name and the word why. When she finally stopped, collapsing into a sobbing ball wrapped around her daughter, one of the townsmen passing by in a buckboard stopped. They helped William get his wife and daughter in the back and the man gently drove the broken family home.

The funeral for little Audie was held two days later. Mildred had been quietly buried in the opposite corner of the cemetery the morning after the bodies had been discovered. But it had been a near thing. Nathan Wright's popularity had extended well beyond the grave and several of the townspeople—who the marshal knew to be kind, gentle folk—had gathered outside the doctor's office that evening, demanding that he turn over Mildred's body to them.

"She doesn't deserve burying," shouted an anonymous voice from deep within the growing mob. "Burn her to ash and scatter her to the wind!"

The old doctor stood guard at his door. Nearly all of these people were good friends, had been for years, but on this night he feared for his very own life at their hands. And while he might understand their anger, while there was a small part of him that might very much want to do just what they were calling for, he would not let them desecrate her. At least not without a fight that would force them to do so over his dead body.

The marshal had feared something like this might occur and had quickly moved in between the doctor and the mob.

"Go home, people," he shouted. "Go on home. There's nothing for you here. Go home."

"We aim to burn that witch, marshal, and we can make this a necktie party too if you want."

The marshal's blood turned cold. He'd start shooting if he had to, if the crowd moved for the door, and no matter who he shot, it would be a very good friend. But he, like the doctor, had a duty to perform. He slid his hand down to his pistol, praying he wouldn't have to draw it from its holster. He knew if that gun came out, there would be more than two bodies to bury. He started to shout out another command to go home and was surprised to hear another man's voice instead of his own when he opened his mouth.

"I am ashamed of all of you," thundered Pastor Jim Hall and every head in the crowd turned to look to the rear where an angry man glared back at them. "A young woman lies dead in there and I've just come from a house where a young girl lies dead, her family torn asunder. They are all of them God's children and you want to spill more blood, bring more grief and misery to this terrible day.

"Have you no shame," Pastor Jim thundered, an angry man who had never been known to have shown anger in public before. He pushed his way through to the front of the crowd and snatched a butcher knife right out of the hand of one startled man. "Is that what you want, Joseph Keta, more bloodshed? Then here, take this blade and spill mine. No? How about you, Howard Rogers? Or you, John Clarkson? No? Then go home, all you, and pray God sends you some human compassion on this foul night, for all of you are so sorely lacking in it that it pains me to call you my flock."

Just as quickly as it had gathered, the crowd melted away into the night without another word and the marshal drew his hand away from his gun with a heavy sigh of relief.

"Thank you, Pastor."

"All in the Lord's work, son," the pastor replied as he laid his shaking hand on the marshal's shoulder. "Well, we have failed to save the body, let us see if we can do a better job of it for her poor soul. I will pray for her tonight and I suggest we conduct a very quick burial at first light."

The pastor had stayed with Mildred through the night and, as soon as enough daylight allowed them to see what they were about, solemnly read over her remains after the simple coffin had been lowered into the hastily dug grave. The doctor, the marshal and the two grave diggers were the only mourners for Mildred. They would fashion a plain marker for her later, after the town's passions had cooled off to a safer level for everyone.

By contrast, the funeral for Audie would bring in every single resident in the county just one day later. Elizabeth had sat silent vigil next to her daughter every minute that passed, from the time the marshal had handed her into her arms until they came to carry the child away to her final resting place. William had stood at the head of her casket, so still he might have been taken for a statue.

What had once been a happy home filled with vibrant people, laughter and love was now overshadowed by darkness and occupied by the grim specters of the people who had once resided there. Elizabeth remained inconsolable. William, gaunt and haggard, ready to explode at the slightest provocation in one instant, only to have the fire vanish almost as quickly as it had arisen to sink silently back into his shell of stone.

The Fergusons had come down from Atlanta as soon as word of the tragedy had reached them. They too had lost a child early in its life and knew the pain the young couple were in all too well. While Mrs. Ferguson did what she could for Elizabeth, her husband took William aside.

"William," he began earnestly. "There are things of much more value than a railroad or a shipping empire. Family is one of them. There is nothing here for either of you, in LaGrange or even in the whole of Georgia itself, but ghosts and painful memories.

"Take Elizabeth and go west, son," he continued. "My brother-in-law, Frederick, has set up his business out in San Francisco and he needs good men like you for his company. As much as I want you with me here, as much as my company needs a man like you, I think it would be better for the both of you to start anew, somewhere far away from here. You're both young still. You can build a fine life, a fine family for yourselves, out there."

"We can't just leave Audie all alone here..." William began.

"She won't be alone, son," Ferguson interrupted kindly but firmly. "She'll be right here, next to her grandparents. I promise you that I'll see to it that all three graves are well tended too. Fresh flowers every day, son, like she was my very own child, you have my word on that."

It had made sense to William and while Elizabeth hadn't enthusiastically said yes, she did not say no either. So William spent that dreadful winter getting their affairs in order, selling their house, transferring clients to another attorney, a young man from Atlanta looking to establish a new practice much like William had, and settling their accounts.

By February, as winter began to release its grip, they were at last ready to go. A covered wagon packed with supplies and those personal items and clothes that they had decided to take with them to the West. The house, along with all of its furnishings, had been purchased at a hefty sum by the Fergusons. They had promised to sell it all back to the couple for the sum of one dollar should the Caldwells ever desire to return to LaGrange.

"Think of it as a farewell present, in every sense of the word, son," Mr. Ferguson had said when William protested that it would be as much as stealing if he only paid them one dollar back in return.

William and Elizabeth had made their final farewells at the gravesides of their daughter and Elizabeth's parents. Neither of them so much as casted a single glance over in the direction where Mildred lay. Her grave was still unmarked all these months later and many in the town had begun to wonder aloud if a marker would ever be placed for her at all. Then, with nearly the entire town gathered nearby, William helped Elizabeth up into the wagon, then stepped up in the seat himself and gathered up the reins. He paused to say goodbye, to thank them all for their help through the difficult times he and his wife had endured. But he could not find the words, nor could any of those gathered around. Finally, he raised a hand in farewell then, with a flick of the reins, started the wagon westward.

It took them nearly a month to make the trek over to Benton County, Arkansas. It was there where the wagon trains bound for the western lands would gather for the journey each spring. Once in Benton County, they had joined in with the Baker-Fancher Party, a large train, that would see them to California where the new job and a new home awaited their arrival in San Francisco. Elizabeth had remained quiet and withdrawn since the day of Audie's death. But shortly after their crossing of the Mississippi River on a ferry into eastern Arkansas, she had begun to improve somewhat. It was as if crossing that wide river had somehow washed away some of the evil that had descended upon them both. Even William felt somewhat changed within by it.

The train left Arkansas shortly after the couple had arrived, crossing into Kansas and eventually made its way into the Utah territory. They had arrived in Salt Lake City in late August, the final restock of supplies before pushing across the Sierras and into California before the snow started falling. By then, Elizabeth had been riding on the seat next to William and marveled at the new, wild landscapes they traversed. It was hard work to hold the reins and keep his arm around his wife at the same time, but William didn't mind that effort at all, especially when he saw his wife smiling for the first time in a very long time. Ferguson had been right. The move west was just what they both had needed so very badly.

The train departed Salt Lake City, turning south to follow the trail of all of the past trains that had made this journey. Several days later, the train had passed Cedar City and had intended to stop for a day or so at Mountain Meadows. But the Caldwell's wagon had other ideas that day. A bolt, that had kept the wagon firmly connected to the axel, had sheared off and would need to be replaced or the wagon would eventually come apart. An hour or two of work at the most, but they would be well behind the train for that time period until they eventually caught up.

"You folks all right, Will?" Solomon Wood asked as he rode up to the wagon on one of the finest Palomino's William had ever seen.

"Yes, Sol," William answered from under the wagon where he'd been inspecting the damage. "I can fix it right up; it will just take me a couple of hours to get this done."

"Need some help?"

"No, we'll be fine, thank you. We'll catch up with you at the Meadows," William replied.

"Okay," Wood answered, booting his mount gently to get it moving forward. "I'll send word along to Mr. Fancher and we'll send some boys back for you if you don't roll in before too long. So long, Will, Mrs. Caldwell."

Wood tipped his hat to Elizabeth then rode off to keep pace with the still-moving train. In a mere few minutes, the Caldwells found themselves all alone on the trail.

As it turned out, it had only taken William just over an hour to make the needed repair. But when he'd finished it, lying there in the prairie grass in the shade of the wagon, he had caught sight of Elizabeth sitting next to him, just looking at him. Before he could say a word to her, she quickly leaned down and kissed him in a way she hadn't done in a very long time. Which was why they were well over two hours, and likely closer to three hours, behind the back end of the train once their wagon had finally resumed its trek for Mountain Meadows that day.

It would be a close thing, getting to the Meadows before night fell, and the rest of the party would probably have already sent along a few riders to scout the back trail to look for them except for one small detail. The entire wagon train was under attack, besieged by what looked like Piute Indians. But both William and Elizabeth noticed at least two white men intermixed with the attackers about the same time those very same men had noticed the arrival of one more wagon.

The entire party below was fully under siege and there was no way for the Caldwells to get through the attackers. Knowing there was nothing he could do to help those below, and with a yell that would make any Southerner proud, William turned loose his team and made a run to get away from the scene with four of the attackers quickly falling in behind them in pursuit.

The daughter of Nathan Wright had been raised to handle such situations as well. Will's full attention was needed on driving the wagon. Her task was to defend it. In addition to a pair of fully loaded pistols, the wagon also carried a Springfield rifled musket. Her father had taught her all too well how to fire, reload and fire again, and to do so very quickly. More importantly, he had taught her to make every shot count.

The first two pursuers never got close to the wagon. The third she dispatched with the Springfield even as the remaining rider opened fire on the wagon. That last rider made the mistake of jumping into the wagon. The Colt Navy pistol fired once and launched the man right back out the way he'd entered. Seeing no additional pursuit, she made her way back to the front of the wagon.

"I think we can slow down now," she said. "I don't see anyone else behind us."

Unconvinced, William shook his head and kept going at full speed for another hour until the exhausted horses had to stop.

"I think we lost them," William said as he pulled the team to a halt. He stood up and started to get down from the wagon. But instead of lightly jumping down to the ground, he pitched forward and struck the ground hard. That was when Elizabeth saw the blood on the wagon seat where he'd been sitting.

"Will!" she screamed and scrambled down to her fallen husband. Rolling him over onto his back, she found two bullet wounds on the right side and low. She quickly set about stopping the bleeding.

"Elizabeth," William's voice was weak, his breathing labored and it was an effort for him to talk. "You've got to leave me here and keep on going. There may be more following."

"I'm not leaving you here like this," Elizabeth exclaimed, realizing that one of the bullets had punctured a lung and she was not equipped at all to do anything about it.

"I'm sorry," William rasped, weakly reaching up to gently touch her face. Then his hand dropped bonelessly back to the ground. "I'm sor…"

"Will?"

But he would not respond to her again, not in this life at any rate. Defeated by this latest loss, just when it seemed life was worth living once again, Elizabeth spent the rest of the night holding her dead husband's head in her lap. She didn't care if more men had followed them and killed her too once they found her.

But when the sun finally lifted above the peaks in the eastern sky, she was still sitting there. No one had come and it seemed that none would come. Stiff from sitting for so long in one position, still shivering slightly from the night's cold air, she gently laid William's head onto the ground and rose to her feet. In their haste to flee the assault on the train, she had lost track of what direction Will had turned their wagon during the pursuit. He had almost immediately gotten off the trail and the area behind the wagon where he had finally stopped was covered in tall grass as far as she could see, so there were no wagon tracks for her to follow. She literally had no idea how to get back to where they'd last seen the other wagons. Assuming that returning to that terrible scene was even a safe option for her to attempt.

Nor did she know where any nearby towns or settlements might be located. All she had was a general sense of direction and a choice of four possible directions to take from here. She decided she would hold a westerly course as much as the terrain would allow until she found someone who could help her.

She could not leave Will's body exposed to the elements and any scavengers. So she rolled him over twice until his body was up against a cut in the ground where no grass had grown, carved out no doubt by some long ago rainfall. She then used a shovel to collapse the wall of earth until it covered him completely. Taking off her scarf, she tightly tied it to the shovel handle and drove the blade as hard as she could into the ground to mark his grave so she could find him again once she had located help. Emotionally drained and thoroughly exhausted, she climbed up into the wagon and urged the horses to start moving.

Four dreadfully long days passed by and she hadn't yet spotted a single sign of human activity. She began to suspect that she was no longer holding a westerly course and had even began to fear that she was now hopelessly lost. Her greatest dread now was that she was likely going in circles and might have been doing so for at least a day, if not longer.

But, early in the morning of the fifth day, she at last spotted a large building in the distance. It stood alone in the middle of a barren stretch of land but at that moment, it was the loveliest thing she had ever seen in her entire life. She drove the team up to the building but became concerned that she hadn't seen anyone moving about. It did not seem abandoned. The three-story building looked almost brand new, the wooden planks coated in fresh yellow paint. Above a set of black doors was a sign.

Infinity Hotel.

Just as she drew the team to a halt, an older man in hat and a heavy topcoat that seemed out of place here, stepped out of the doorway.

"Dear me, child," the old man exclaimed as he looked up at her. "You look about all done in."

"Our wagon train was attacked several days ago," Elizabeth explained. "My husband was killed. I need someone to go back with me and get him."

"Of course, my dear, of course," the old man replied, holding out a hand to help her down. "But it will be a few days before anyone will be able to accompany you. Let's get you inside. You could use some rest in a good bed, a decent meal and a bath, I'd wager."

"My horses and wagon…" Elizabeth began.

"I'll tend to them, my dear," the old man soothed. "We have a very nice stable and good hay for them; your wagon will be safe, I promise. Go on inside, dear, and leave them to me."

She couldn't deny that the thought of a hot meal, a bath and a soft bed was appealing. So she walked up to the black doors and pushed them open. As she crossed the threshold, she felt a slight chill but passed it off as exhaustion and let the doors swing closed behind her.

She walked up to the front desk, impressed with the lobby. It certainly surpassed the hotel she and Will had stayed in while they had been in Atlanta. The man behind the counter turned around as she stepped up. It was the manager.

"Welcome to the Infinity Hotel, ma'am," he said with a smile. "We'll take good care of you for as long as you are here."

ELEVEN

I had listened to her tell her story without comment. That every single word of it was the absolute truth I never doubted, not even for a second. I admired her inner strength and marveled how anyone could keep on going despite the never-ending series of blow after blow falling on her like she had. I wasn't so sure that I would have been able to do the same in her position.

Sadly, I knew that I was about to deliver one more blow to her. Because the telling of her incredible story would result in just one outcome: a question that she would ask. The only question she could ask. And it was a question that I had the answer to.

"It was the middle of September when I walked through those doors," Elizabeth said quietly, as if she already braced herself for what was coming. "The year was eighteen fifty-seven. I know some great amount of time has had to have passed since then, but I don't know exactly how much. What was the day and year when you and Mr. Womack arrived here?"

I hesitated and she immediately picked up on it. As much as I didn't want to tell her, she deserved an answer and to delay any longer would only be cruel.

"When Charlie and I got here, the year was two thousand and nineteen."

Her eyes widened and the blood drained from her face. Where the blood went I couldn't tell because every inch of exposed skin, and there was quite a lot thanks to her uniform, had turned bone white.

"One hundred and sixty-two years," she said so quietly I could barely hear her. She had probably been thinking only a few years had passed, maybe even a decade or two at most. But certainly nothing close to over a century and a half of time that had gone by while she had been trapped within. I tried to think of something to say to make it easier for her. But there simply weren't any words, at least none that existed in my vocabulary.

But there was something I could do. As the magnitude of it finally hit her, she began to shake. I went over to her and drew her close, letting her know she was not alone in this and offering her whatever comfort and support she needed.

She buried her head in my shoulder and it was not too long after that the tears came in harsh, racking sobs. I did the only thing I could do in the situation, just held her close and let her cry it out. Sixteen decades trapped inside this place. I had to admit that number hammered at me and I wondered if I would handle it any better if someone were to come along and tell me I'd been here that long. And how much time in fact had passed on the outside since Charlie and I had entered that lobby below? What was the ratio of elapsed time inside to outside? For all I knew, a decade could have already slipped by out there. I filed that terrible thought away for later. It didn't matter right now as long as we had no way back out.

She finally quieted and the shaking subsided. I waited for her to pull away but she stayed put, head against my shoulder and clutching my arms tightly as if she feared what would happen if she let go. Not that I was complaining, of course. Still, I was willing to stay there for as long as she wanted and needed me to.

Maybe it was a little gallows humor, the very human reaction to a situation beyond any understanding, that made me say the first words out of my mouth after what seemed to be a few minutes had passed.

"For what it's worth, you don't look a day over a hundred to me."

I was rewarded with a sort of half-chuckle, half-snort of someone who'd been through hell and against all explanation could still laugh in the Devil's face and spit in his eye for good measure. She pulled her head back then, but only by a few inches, and sniffled in a way that made me wish that men of my era still made carrying a handkerchief a standard dressing accessory as she reached up to wipe away an errant tear from her cheek.

She started to say something then but stopped as our eyes met. I had come to realize, as I had sat there holding her, that if I had met her back in Denver that this would be the woman I would move heaven and Earth for to spend the rest of my days with. All of those girls I had spent time with were just that, girls—shallow things that paled in comparison to this woman I'd found here in this living hell.

Maybe that was what had stopped her from speaking for I am sure she saw all of that in my eyes at that moment. I say I was sure because it was what I saw when I looked into hers. I doubt any man would hesitate for a second to sell his soul just to have a woman look at him the way she was at me then. Had a man in a red suit magically appeared in front of me with a contract and a pen in his hand at that moment, I would have signed it without a moment of hesitation.

I couldn't say which of us moved toward the other first or even if we both moved at the same time. But once our lips met, there was no doubt where we'd be moving next.

I won't tell you that clothing was ripped away, bosoms heaved or that there was a lot of moaning and the occasional scream—though it turned out that she was a biter so cut me some slack here—or anything else you'd find out of a seedy romance novel. Okay, there was a lot of that the first time around and although the second time was less frenetic, it was certainly no less fulfilling.

But what passed between us in that room was more than just sex, as incredibly hot as it was notwithstanding. It was two people, two souls that needed to be reminded that they were still very much alive and still so very human, no matter how insane the circumstances they found themselves in.

As I lay there on the bed, this amazing woman's head on my chest with her hand resting gently over my heart which now completely belonged to her, I came to a sudden realization. We would never stop trying to find a way to get out of this place, but if it were our fate to spend eternity in here at least we would not have to do it alone.

TWELVE

Elizabeth lay still, listening and feeling the heartbeat of this man she barely knew and yet felt she had known all of her life. She reveled in feeling his chest slowly rise and fall as he breathed, in the feel of her naked body intertwined with his and in the warmth of his body that fended off the cool air in the room.

She'd been surprised by her reaction to him after the shock of finding out exactly how long she'd been trapped in this place wore off. Unnerved at the depth of the feeling, she had started to withdraw to get her thoughts in some semblance of order only to be surprised again, this time by discovering that he felt the same about her when she'd looked into his eyes.

She had never felt this way about a man before, not even Will had brought about this intensity of desire in her and Will had been a wonderful lover and husband to her during their brief marriage. Though the two men didn't resemble each other at all physically—Will had been a little shorter, slightly more muscular and his hands rougher from working the railroads—they were of a similar character.

But she doubted very much that Will would have been able to avoid the fate that had befallen all of the other guests while Peter, despite briefly teetering on the brink of insanity, had managed to hang onto the reality of their situation. That inner strength attracted her to him almost as much as the physical attraction that she felt.

But there was something else too. In her father's vast library back in LaGrange, she had read stories of old souls, long parted from their past lives together, and constantly struggling across great gulfs of time to reunite with one another. She had always thought they were too fanciful to possibly be true.

And yet here she was with a man she had only just met and yet she felt she was destined to be with and suddenly those fanciful tales were no longer so silly to her. They had been brought together for a reason and she very much wanted that reason to be to find a way out for themselves and for the others helplessly trapped in here.

But first, there was something else she wanted the two of them to accomplish. Her hand slowly drifted southward and she felt a little thrill as he responded to her movement.

"Dear lady," he said in mock seriousness, trying to sound like an old Southern gentleman and not quite succeeding. "Whatever are your intentions?"

She lifted her head to look up at him, the coy little smile on her face belying the wicked gleam in her eyes and was imminently pleased to find the same expression on his face. If time no longer ran in here, then they had an eternity to accomplish their ultimate goal.

They might as well make the most of it.

* * * * *

The manager was the only living being in the entire hotel who could still measure the passage of time within these walls. After a fashion of course. He did not age any more than the others inside the Infinity did. But he could still tell how much time *should* have elapsed from one event until the next.

For example, he'd been looking for Elizabeth for the last five hours. He could track which general area she was in on his pad but not a specific location as she did not carry a key card like the guests did. From the front lobby to maintenance area to the casino, he'd followed her, only to fail to actually see her with his own eyes at any of those places.

Then she turned up alone in Mr. Childress' room and that brought him up short. To his recollection, she had never ventured into any guest's room before. So he simply waited and watched his pad until Childress' hasty arrival in his room from the park area. The reason for Childress' haste was also known to the manager.

He waited some more as two hours passed.

Even though he could not actually see what the two of them were doing, there really was only one explanation that he could think of—given his understanding of human nature in general as well as these two people in particular—for why they would remain in that room for that length of time.

She had never done that with any other guest either, not even the last most likely candidate that had come through three decades or real time ago. As the minutes continued to tick by with the pair still in the room, the manager dared to do the one thing he'd feared he had forgotten how to do in all the centuries that had passed unnoticed by the others in here.

He began to believe again.

THIRTEEN

The one thing about the way we were going was that it made me understand why all of the other people in here had seemingly surrendered themselves to this place. If one set aside the horror of being forever trapped within its walls, and focused instead on its Garden of Eden-like enticements, it was actually a very great temptation.

I would be lying if I told you that the thought of staying in this bed for all of eternity next to this woman and forever forsaking the real world outside wasn't something that I could easily do and probably never regret. I suppose some of the others, and quite possibly every single one of them when it came right down to it, had faced this moment of decision in their own way and found the temptation too great to resist, if they'd even consciously realized they'd made the decision at all.

But as tempting as this particular Garden of Eden was to me, it wasn't the world we'd been born to, it wasn't where we belonged. And it was that sense of being out of place which was why we had to break free of this trap and soon. Meaning we had some important issues to work out.

Which would be very hard to do with Liz's wandering hands serving as one of those quite numerous and very enticing distractions. I was about to remark that sixteen decades of celibacy certainly seemed to be an extremely effective aphrodisiac. Then I thought better of it and tossed it in the mental wastebasket where idiotic flippant remarks like that belonged and got to work on what needed our attention.

"That door out there," I said aloud with a quick nod of my head toward the faraway wall beyond the back door of my room. "Even if it isn't the direct exit out of here, it may eventually lead us to the way out. It's important enough to have a very forceful deterrent standing guard over it so there's something behind it that's worth trying for at the very least."

"That makes sense," she said. "But just how are you planning to get past that monster out there? As far as I know, this place doesn't have an armory. Not that I think there's a gun big enough to scratch him, much less slow him down."

And there was that out-of-time displacement again. She'd missed so much of history being trapped within these walls for so long. The Civil War was still a couple of years away when she'd come here. While the munitions of her time might not have worked on that beast out there, the human race had done a pretty good job at improving its weaponry. A nuclear device—while likely overkill—would do the job so I was sure that there were a few weapons of my time that would put him down for the count.

Unfortunately, none of them were handy and I very much doubted I would find any material inside here to throw together anything stronger than a flyswatter. Making a mental note to make sure I was properly armed the next time I found myself ensnared in a trap like this, I scoured my brain for a solution to the problem.

Ensnared.

"What?" Liz asked, seeing the look on my face. "What's wrong?"

I didn't answer at first as I tried to remember the landscape around that door. The lake and the path to the door and its vicious guardian were clearly imprinted on my brain. But what I tried to recall was the layout approaching the door, namely, just exactly how tall and flexible those two trees nearest the door had been and exactly how they were positioned relative to the lake.

"Liz," I asked when I felt sure I had my answer. "Do you think we can find a couple of very lengthy ropes somewhere in this hotel?"

"Ropes?" she replied, puzzled. "Are we going to try to tie him up?"

"Actually," I said with a slight smile, "I was thinking we can send him on a nice little trip."

I filled her in on the finer details of what I had planned and she confirmed the availability of one or two necessary items to make it work. With our goal firmly set, we got to work, delayed only by what should have been a quick shower had we done so separately but would not nearly have been as much fun. So we took about twice as long with that task before dressing and heading out into the hotel in search of supplies.

Finding the rope topped the list, because without it or something similar, there would be no need to locate the rest until we figured out what our next move was. Liz led the way to the second floor—a level completely dedicated to maintenance and inaccessible to the guests—and fortunately for us, no one was around.

After a few minutes of rummaging around the boxes and shelves, we found several coils of rope in varying lengths. Trying to guesstimate in my head the distances involved and adding in a little extra just to be safe, I found two lengths that looked to be just about right.

Taking them in hand, and quickly collecting a small but razor-sharp hatchet and a pair of leather work gloves lying nearby, I walked over to a pile of empty canvas bags and picked out one of the larger bags. After tossing in the coils of rope, the hatchet and the gloves, I grabbed a pair of medium-sized bags and threw them in with the rest of the items.

"What are those for?"

"Just in case it takes us a long time to find the way out after we get past the door," I replied. "Or if we get outside and find ourselves out in the middle of nowhere. We might find ourselves needing a change of clothes and some food and water."

She nodded and then reached down to pluck something off one of the workbenches.

"We might need this too," she said, handing me a ragged block of chalk. "So we don't find ourselves lost or going in circles if that door doesn't open directly to the outside. Or to find our way back, if it turns out to be a dead end."

That was good thinking and I gratefully took the chalk and added it, and three small flashlights that I discovered, to the bag. It was there, in the set of her face, the dread we both felt at that particular scenario. That we would go out that door and discover that it did not lead to the outside world.

"If we do have to come back inside," I said softly, "then we continue searching for the way out until we have exhausted every possibility."

"And then?"

"Then we play our last card," I answered. "We'll have nothing to lose, no fear of discovery at that point. So we'll just confront our friend the manager with what we know and demand to be released."

"Why don't we do that now?"

"If we did, do you think he would let us go?" I asked and waited for her to shake her head in the negative. "Me neither. And then he'd know we were on to this place and maybe he'd be able to stop us from ever getting out of here. Maybe even to the point where we'd be just like all of the others and never want to leave.

"No," I continued. "We leave that as our last move to make when it won't matter any longer if he discovers that we aren't like the rest of the guests."

"And if he won't let us go?" Liz asked, her voice quivering. "Peter, I don't want to live like this forever."

Suicide, she said without actually coming out and saying it. And her point was a valid one for wouldn't death be better than the living death that eternity trapped in here presented? Yet, the thought of seeing Liz lying dead with my own eyes, or even worse having even had a hand in her death, sent a sharp pain across my chest that I never again wanted to experience.

The true horror of this place struck me then. What if we found out that Liz's original thought had been right all along? That we had in fact already died and that even the hope of suicide as an escape from here would be denied us. That we would find ourselves with the choice that was not a choice at all.

An eternity in limbo in full awareness with the knowledge of no possible release, or a complete surrender of whatever that "spark" of awareness was that made us individuals for the sake of not having to bear the brunt of the pain that knowledge of the inescapable trap would bring. Which, I wondered, was the lesser of these two evils?

I could see Liz's thoughts had traveled along the same desolate path as mine and she had no better answer than did I.

"We'll cross that bridge when, and if, we have to," I said, giving myself a firm mental shake. "For now, we have an option that might get us out of here. Let's get to it."

Picking up the large bag, I slung the strap across my shoulder and we headed for our next shopping stop, the laundry. We filled one of the medium bags with several changes of clothes, underwear and socks in our sizes for each of us. Rigging up the bag as a makeshift backpack, I helped Liz shoulder it on.

"How is the weight?" I asked as I adjusted my own bag to get the balance right. "It's not pulling too much to one side or throwing off your balance, is it?"

"No," she answered, shifting her shoulders a little until the straps settled on them to her liking. "This is fine."

We headed for our final stop, food and water. We found plenty of water bottles, enough to get us by for several days if we were careful. I was hoping for energy bars but wasn't surprised that none were to be found. We could easily carry enough of them with us to last for a long time without having to lug around a lot of dead weight, making them ideal for our situation.

But in their absence, I had to be choosy and wise with what we could take. It had to last, had to be easily opened and closed, and it had to keep us alive. I settled for a lot of dried fruit and nuts, a few chocolate bars and every scrap of jerked meat inside of a container that I discovered at the very last minute.

It wouldn't be fine dining and we'd have to ration to be safe, but it would keep us going for as long as we needed it to. More importantly, it all fit into the last empty bag and it wasn't heavy enough when I picked it up to be of a concern. We were on the way out of the storage area when I spotted one last item we just might need. Snatching the first aid kit off of the wall, I stuffed it into Liz's bag.

"All right, I think that will do it. Let's go take care of our furry friend and get the hell out of here."

All the way back up to my room, I worried that the manager would suddenly appear and shut us down before we even got started. I wasn't concerned with the guests we passed as they would see nothing abnormal and in fact, they all went about their business without a word.

With a deep sigh of relief, from both of us, we slipped into my room and shut the door. Liz immediately headed for the exit to the park while I paused just long enough to grab my cell phone and slipped it into my pocket. There was no way to know exactly how much real time had passed outside or where we'd appear once we got out. Hopefully the thing would still be able to place a call for help.

I had just stepped out into the park when a sudden thought brought me up short and I turned around and just stood there, looking back into the room.

"Peter, what's wrong?"

"Charlie," I said, turning my head to look back at her. "What if we get out but can't get help to get back inside for the others? He'll be trapped here. Forever."

Liz walked over slowly and placed her hand on my shoulder.

"He's my friend, Liz."

"I know."

"If I go back for him, he won't want to come with us, will he?"

"No, he won't."

"And if I try to force him, there will be a scene and the manager will know something's up and I might not get back here myself."

"Yes."

I leaned my head against the doorway and closed my eyes, hating this place. Hating the decision I was about to make because it was the only possible one to make.

"I can't pull him out with us right now, can I?"

"No, Peter, you can't. I'm so very sorry."

I'd never heard so much sorrow in one person's voice before and I never wanted to hear it again if I could avoid it. Silently, I swore I'd do whatever I could to find a way to get back here and free these people, every single one of them. And hopefully somewhere along the line I'd find the courage to face my best friend and ask him to forgive me for leaving him behind in a living hell. Knowing I'd never forgive myself if I never found a way to free him, and without another word, I pushed off from the doorway and walked away, leaving my room and my friend behind, hoping the former was permanent and that the latter was only for a brief time. Liz followed quietly, knowing there were no words to help, but also knowing her just being nearby in support was the best thing she could do right now.

We reached the point along the path where those two particular trees that I remembered stood, a pair of impressive shortleaf pines. They had grown up side by side, easily reaching a good sixty feet above the ground, and the small trunks were bare of branches or limbs for the first thirty feet.

They were sturdy enough to bear a sizeable load of weight while still flexible enough to bend over without snapping in half. A perfect natural catapult to send the impediment to our escape on a very long flight indeed, provided of course that I could shimmy my way up the first bare trunk and tie off the end of the long rope to it. Then make my way over to the second tree and tie it together with the first without falling and breaking my neck.

I rigged up the smaller rope to use as a sling to loop around the tree trunk and then around my back to brace against as I worked my way up the trunk. Wishing I had better shoes for the task, I dug in each foot as best I could and pushed up, easing the tension on the rope just enough to allow for the upward motion. Then, when it felt like I'd gone as high as I could, I leaned back into the rope and dug my feet back into the trunk to keep from losing ground.

It was hard going, and a couple of times I nearly mistimed my leap and lean routine, but with a great sense of relief, and completely drenched in sweat, I made it to the lower branches and pulled myself up into the canopy. Standing on a pair of thick branches that easily held my weight, I rested for a few moments and heard Liz cheering me on from below.

I tied off the rope to the tree and dropped the tail of it down toward the ground. One tug and the rope would untie, something we'd need to do so that our huge friend would keep going in the right direction once we got him airborne instead of having him rebounding back, something he'd definitely do if he remained tied to these two trees.

Gathering up the rest of the rope, I tossed it across to the second tree and thankfully the loops all got hung up in the branches and did not fall back to the ground below. Now came the fun part. Down below, the trees were barely six feet apart but up here, it looked more like sixty as I prepared to jump across.

Even knowing that whatever damage I would do would quickly be repaired if I should come up short, it was still a hard thing to do, hurling myself out into open air with a four-story fall to the ground, waiting if I missed my target.

But it would still be a lot easier than working my way back down this tree and then back up the other one. So I planted my feet and pushed off as hard as I could, aiming for an open point in the canopy of the other tree where I'd tossed the rope.

I hit my target, more or less, and the cuts and scratches of the branches along with the pain where my left shoulder slammed into the trunk of the tree quickly passed. More important to the matter at hand, I hung on to the trunk and did not fall. It took a few seconds for me to catch my breath after the impact with the tree had pushed it all out and then I grabbed the rope and hauled, hand over hand, until the tops of the two trees' trunks were nearly touching.

With a floor of branches to walk on, I worked my way out to the midpoint and tied off the rope to keep the trees in place and let the rest of the rope drop down to the ground. With a couple of final tugs to make sure the knots would hold where needed, I repelled down the rope to the ground below and happily found myself in Liz's arms.

"Are you okay?"

"Yeah," I said, in no particular hurry to change my present circumstance. "But remind me never to do something like that again."

"I will. So what's next?"

"We've got our catapult," I said, reluctantly pulling away from our embrace. "Now we need to set it and lay down the snares."

Grabbing hold of the hanging rope, and using a large boulder as a crude block and tackle, we pulled the trees over as far as we could. While I held the line taut, Liz tied off the rope to a nearby tree and did such a good job of it that when I let go of the rope, the bent-over trees barely moved an inch. I tested the line and found it so tight I could have played a concerto on it if I'd had a bow handy. When that line was cut, whatever was attached to it would move in a new direction and in a very big hurry.

Taking the smaller rope that I'd used as a sling earlier, I fashioned a pair of loops and placed them in two likely places where our quarry would pass through when he chased the bait. If the timing was right, he'd get caught in one of the loops and be on his way.

I had assumed that I would be the bait, letting him chase me through this point and having Liz cut the line but she had other ideas.

"You have a better idea of how this works and when to cut the line," she remarked when I started to show her where to cut the line. "I was a fast runner when I was a little girl and I can still run pretty fast for my age so I'll lead him to the snares."

Now, I was just enough of a male chauvinist deep inside to confirm that her statement did not go over well with me. She patiently waited out my protestations, which were quite loud and even more pointed. She then invited me to come up with a better idea.

As I watched her approach the door and its malevolent guardian from my perch atop the boulder just inches away from the rope, gripping the hatchet hard enough to leave an indention in the handle, I still hadn't come up with a better plan. Nor had I begun to like seeing her there in harm's way anymore than I had when she'd first proposed it. But all I could do was stand there and watch, and sweat it out, all the while fully prepared to dash off in her direction if that damned blue beast caught up to her.

I knew throwing the hatchet at him was probably as likely to damage him as spitting in his eye, but I couldn't just stand there and watch him claw her to pieces without doing something.

At first, it looked like nothing would happen at all as she walked right up to the door without there being so much as a tremor from the blue and brown mound. But then, as it had happened earlier with me, all hell broke loose as soon as she grasped the handle and started to open the door.

The bear reared up with a snarl and Liz stood there gaping at it for a lot longer than I liked. But just as I started to yell at her to get moving, she bolted away and the bear charged after her. There had been one heart-stopping moment as the bear got in one swipe that had just missed her by the slightest of margins. But despite that close call, she ran him right into the snares.

As soon as she had cleared them, he had just started to step down into the first loop and I hammered the blade into the rope, taking out a huge chunk of the rock beneath it. The rope let go with a loud twang and whipped into the air, pulling the loop tight around the bear's leg and launching him skyward with a mighty bellow. Just as the two trees snapped back into their upright position, I pulled the other end of the rope, untying the knot around the first tree so it would not stop the beast from flying away when he hit the end of the rope.

The last we saw of the bear he was still gaining altitude with all of the ropes trailing freely behind him. It also sounded like his howls also gained in intensity as he flew away and I took some small perverse pleasure in that. After the beating he'd given me earlier, even though they had all quickly healed, I found it hard to feel the least bit sorry for him.

Fearful of a back-up system, we wasted no time celebrating. Gathering up our bags of supplies and clothing, we hustled to the now open door and dashed inside, slamming it shut behind us. We stood there hugging each other then, each trying to catch our breath after our exertions, laughing like maniacs as we finally allowed ourselves a small celebration.

"We did it," Liz exclaimed. "We did it!"

Yes, we had done it. We had gotten out of the hotel proper. Now, I thought to myself as I turned to see what lay beyond, we needed to see exactly to where it was that we had gotten ourselves.

FOURTEEN

The manager had always considered himself to be a patient man. After all, he had entered into this situation with the full understanding that it would be a very long one to endure at that. But there had been more than a few times over his stay when he had feared that his time here would never come to an end, that he would never be free of this place.

The sad fact was that if he was indeed condemned to this fate, he would not utter one word of complaint. There was no one person, or entity, that he could pass off the blame to for his present circumstance save one. Himself.

So he had marshalled every bit of self-discipline that he possessed and did the only thing he could do. Wait. For however long it took, even if relief never came. He would wait.

But it wasn't easy, especially now when it seemed that the end of his torment might finally be at hand. Every fiber of his being wanted to leap out of his office chair and find out exactly what Liz and Peter were up to.

Why had they left Peter's room and headed straight for the maintenance floor, then to the laundry and on to food storage before returning to his room? What were they up to? He desperately tried to piece together what he knew with what he knew about them to get a clue to their intentions.

Were they planning on going somewhere specific? Were they thinking they could hide somewhere in the hotel? Were they going to commandeer a room and try to hold out?

He'd been onto Liz from the start. Clearly, she alone had remained aware that the Infinity was not what it seemed to all of the other guests. He had not let her know this of course, any more than he would let her know that while she was the key to their mutual salvation, they must await the arrival of one more person.

He had to admit that Peter looked more and more like that person. But this was a fact that was still yet to be proven and there was only one way to do that. Sit back, observe and wait. So, even as he monitored their movements about the hotel, he tended to the requirements of his routine within these walls.

But when they immediately exited Peter's room and made their way into the central park, he knew he could not sit back and wait any longer. He had a very good idea what their next destination was now, but could not quite figure out how they planned to get past the guardian to reach that door.

Whatever it was, he wanted to see it, and the results, for himself. So he quickly made his way to the central park, entering near a vantage point where he could see the door and its guardian—had the guardian been there that is. The door remained closed and did not look like it had recently been open from what he could see.

Was he too late? Had the attempt already been made, and failed, and were the pair now retreating with the guardian in deadly pursuit?

Just then he heard a loud swooshing sound of air swiftly passing through branches and leaves—or vice versa for all he could tell—and saw two large trees snap back into their natural upright positions. This was quickly followed by the guardian soaring overhead, with ropes trailing behind. The manager tracked the guardian all the way to its landing point and winced in sympathy as it slammed through the farthest wall and, fortunately, ended up inside an unoccupied room.

He looked back just in time to see Liz and Peter, each carrying packs, dashing for the now unguarded door, open it and scurry inside before slamming it shut behind them. The manager took in the scene for a moment, leaned his head back and roared in delighted laughter.

"Brilliant," he exclaimed, still chuckling. "Absolutely brilliant work, Mr. Childress."

Without another look back at the defeated guardian, the manager headed for the door himself and even though there was still much to do, he walked with a great sense of relief. No one else had ever gotten this far, and while there was no guarantee that Childress would make it the rest of the way, it was looking very promising at this point.

Just one more test to pass, Peter, the manager thought to himself as he neared the door, *one last hurdle to clear and then its home free. For all of us.*

The manager pulled open the door, certain the couple had already moved along and were out of sight by now, and found himself praying that young Mr. Childress was the man they needed him to be to get past that final barrier.

As the manager pulled the door shut behind him, he wondered if there were any gods out there that would hear his prayer. And if there was, would there even be one among them that was capable of the quality of mercy needed to answer a prayer from the likes of him.

FIFTEEN

As it turned out, we needn't have bothered bringing the flashlights. When we turned away from the door, we found ourselves in a cave of what looked like solid granite. Some kind of luminous material in the rock lit up the interior just well enough to see what lay ahead clearly. It wasn't daylight bright, but we would easily be able to see where we were going and what lay ahead of us for quite some distance.

The air seemed reasonably fresh and while it wasn't cold, the temperature in the cave was just slightly chilly. Once we started walking, we'd likely not even feel anything but comfortable.

With only one direction for us to take and no reason to linger at the door, we slung our packs onto our shoulders and headed off. For the longest time, the cave sloped slightly downward with no connecting tunnels or turns of any kind. I started to think we wouldn't need the chalk.

But we finally came upon a T-intersection and I dug out a small piece of the chalk and drew an arrow on the wall pointing back the way we'd come from.

"Just in case we do need to go back," I told Liz when she looked at the mark and then at me with the obvious question in her eyes. "Better we know the route back instead of getting lost and going in circles forever."

She didn't seem convinced, but she didn't raise any additional objections either. I wasn't so sure myself if getting lost and eventually dying of starvation and lack of water here in these tunnels wasn't preferred over what we'd face if we went back. But for now, that possibility could be tabled until we'd exhausted the rest of our options in here.

"So here's the question," I said aloud. "Which direction do we go in now?"

To our left, the tunnel sloped downward at a sharper grade than the one we currently stood in. To the right, a slight upward slant and no other clue whatsoever as to which direction would lead us out of here. The geography of the hotel was not a reliable guide to fix our current position with, but it really was all we had to work with for now. If we had started four floors above ground level, then we'd probably dropped those four floors in height during our trek down this tunnel and maybe even a little more.

Heading further down filled me with a sudden apprehension and that feeling was more than enough to decide the issue for me.

"At every junction, we go up or to the right where possible," I said to Liz. "Agreed?"

"It sounds like as good a pattern to start with as anything else," she agreed.

And so it went for some time. We traversed the length of a tunnel, turned either right or up or both in several cases, marked the way we'd come at each turn and continued on. Occasionally we would come across a turn that left us no choice but to go to the left or head back down.

It was hard to tell if we were going in a general direction overall or in one very large circle. The type and coloring of the rock walls rarely changed and I began to fear we were one more turn away from finding ourselves looking at one of my chalk arrows on the wall.

Then we exited one of the tunnels and found ourselves looking out at a huge limestone cavern. Stalactites dozens of feet in length dangled from the roof of the cavern above a field of stalagmite, boulders and rocks below. I could make out two or three possible exits across the way and I was sure there were probably more to find out there.

"This is going to take a little longer than we thought," Liz said as she looked out at the cavern.

"My dear," I quipped, "you have quite the talent for understatement."

We made our way down to the cavern floor and found an arrangement of rocks and boulders to sit and take a break. Rummaging around the bags, I dug out some food and water and looked around for any clues as to which of the other tunnels to take next while we ate.

I had marked the tunnel we had just exited and as I looked around, I counted another seven tunnels scattered around the cavern. Unless we got very lucky and guessed right the first time, we could be in this maze for a very long time to come. Whatever foresight had directed me to pick up as much food and water as we could carry had served us well. I just hoped it would prove to be enough.

"So where do we go from here?" Liz asked, impatient as I was to get started.

That was a very good question. We didn't have a map to work from and there wasn't anything that separated any one of the exits from the other six. And our pattern of going right or up was blown up with these multiple choices.

So it was down to something as arbitrary as just picking one at random or perhaps just going over to the closest one and see where it would lead.

Random, I felt, could get us good and lost, even with us marking the path we took as we went. No, to me I felt that we had established a pattern of sorts and sticking to it gave us the best chance to find our way back to the outside. I explained my thinking to Liz and she agreed. So we packed up our gear and headed for the nearest tunnel that appeared to go up and right.

But just as we were about to step into the passage, a sudden noise brought us both up short. It sounded a lot to my ear like footsteps, someone was nearby and scrabbling along a rocky floor. Then we heard a low whistling sound, someone was approaching us from one of the many caves and whoever it was, they were whistling some sort of tune. I could not recognize what the tune was but it was definitely coming from a human being.

Uncertain if this person would be friendly to us or not, I waved Liz to join me behind a large boulder and we hid behind it, hoping we had chosen an angle to provide cover as we still weren't sure which cave the sounds were coming from.

We didn't have to wait too long before we found out who our visitor was. An old man, dressed up like an old miner from the gold rush days of Liz's time period, complete with battered hat and a knapsack with mining tools dangling from it, appeared in one of the cave openings on the far side of the cavern. Hidden behind the boulder and in the shadows, we could see him clearly but it appeared that he could not see us.

"Well, damn," he exclaimed as he looked out at the cavern. "Wrong again."

After a moment, the old man reached back, grabbed his well-used pick out of the loop holding it to his pack and quickly carved a large X into the side of the cave wall that he stood in. When that was done, he replaced the pick in the pack and then made his way down to the cavern floor, very close to where we had just been sitting. He shrugged the pack off his shoulders and set it down on the largest rock, where a nice flat spot had been worn into it over the years.

"Well, nothing to do but have some lunch," he said aloud to himself. "Then we'll try another one and see where she leads. Wouldn't you agree with me, young feller?"

Liz and I exchanged started looks. There was no way he could have seen either of us and he wasn't looking in our direction now either.

"You can come on out, I'm harmless," the old man called out, still not looking in our direction. "Well, mostly I'm not, but you and your lady friend will be safe around old Jack. Why don't you both come on out here so we can talk like civilized folks?"

With a shrug of my shoulders, I nodded for Liz to follow and we stepped out from behind the boulder.

"Now then, that's a lot better," the man said without turning around. "No reason why we can't all be more friendly like, seeing as how we're all stuck in the same predicament."

He finally turned around then and we got a good look at him. He was definitely an old man, a mop of dirty white hair spilling out from underneath a well-worn cowboy hat. He had a full white beard and his left eye was squinted closed, with a scar that ran just above the left brow. His other eye was bright blue and undamaged. He wore a dirty blue calico shirt and jeans, both as worn in appearance as his hat, and large mining boots. If one had wanted to make a poster of what a 1850s gold miner looked like, he would have been the perfect model.

"Well now," he said, taking his hat off quickly, "I can see why you were being cautious there, young feller, with such a lovely woman. My name's Jack Smithfield, it's a pleasure to meet you, ma'am."

He seemed harmless enough at first glance and he could be of some help, as long as he could be trusted. There was nothing outwardly wrong with his appearance, but given what we had just escaped, I wasn't so willing to accept anything at face value any longer. Still, there wasn't any need to be needlessly rude at this point.

"I'm Peter Childress," I said, extending a hand out, which the old man took and vigorously pumped. The man had a pretty good grip for his age. "This is Elizabeth Wright."

"Pleased to meet you, ma'am," he replied with a nod of his head before donning his hat again. "You folks look like you've had a rough go of it. I can imagine the why of it."

"Oh?" Liz asked.

"Sure enough," he said as he resumed laying out his provisions. "You folks found your way out of the Infinity Hotel and found yourself right plumb in the middle of this maze of caves, didn't you?"

"What do you know about the Infinity?" I asked.

"Son, I found myself inside that cursed place not so long ago," the old man replied. "I'd just found me a real nice vein of gold up near Buzzard's Pass. Loaded up as much of it as my mule could pack and then I headed back down the mountain to cash in.

"About halfway down," he continued. "The mother of all storms rolled right up on us. It took me awhile to find shelter so we could ride it out. Well, sir, the rain finally let up but we were still socked in by cold, gray clouds. You couldn't see more than two feet in front of you, it was so thick. Well, Sara, that was my mule's name, by the way, Sara and I decided to try to make our way on down anyway. It shouldn't have taken long, even going slow because of the clouds.

"Seemed like we was walking along forever before we finally broke out of them clouds and when we did, it was no country I'd even laid eyes on before. We were still in the mountains all right, but they all looked different. I couldn't for the life of me figure out how we could have walked so far out of the way. I was just fixin' to turn us back around and go back up when I spotted a building down at the foot of the mountain. Figured my best bet of getting back to where I wanted to be was to head on down and get me some directions."

The old man paused in his narrative to offer us some bread and cheese from his pack. Not wanting to be rude, we accepted but I handed him a bottle of water in return, after cracking open the cap. He gave it a strange look, but twisted the cap the rest of the way off and took a long drink.

"Well, now," he said with a smile. "That's about the best tasting water I've had in a long time. Had to be miserly with how much I use down here until I find the way out. Thanks."

He went to hand the bottle back, but I waved at him to keep it. We had more than enough, at least so I hoped.

"Well," he resumed his story after thanking me again. "We wandered on down and found ourselves out front of the Infinity Hotel. I tied Sara off to the hitching post outside and walked on in. Well, it was a right fine hotel at that, everything a body could want. I was anxious to be on my way but they told me the only way back was unpassable due to the storm and it was getting late in the day so I might as well stay the night and then head on out in the morning.

"I hadn't been in a fancy hotel for a long time and the idea of a nice soft bed was mighty appealing. I made arrangement for them to take care of Sara then headed on up to my room. Only it didn't take me long to realize something wasn't right and that no matter how much time seemed to pass, the next morning never showed up."

I looked over at Liz, his story sounded much like ours did.

"How did you get out of the hotel and in here?" she asked him.

"Once I figured out something was out of order, starting with the fact I couldn't find the door I had used to walk into the place to begin with, I started hunting around for a way out. Finally found me a door near the back of the hotel. It didn't open to a room and I couldn't tell where exactly it led to but I figured it couldn't be any worse than where I was now, so I went back and gathered up my pack, went back to the door and stepped on through, closed the door behind me and never looked back. Found myself in this very cavern with all these cave openings all around. I've been walking through them all trying to find a way back to the outside world."

"Nothing tried to stop you from getting to that door?" I asked the old man, that blue behemoth's claws fresh in my mind.

"No, son," he replied. "No one said so much as a peep. I just walked right up to the door, opened it and walked right in without so much as a by your leave from anyone at all."

"Did you ever meet the hotel's manager?" I asked.

"Can't say as I did, son," he answered. "Only member of the hotel staff I talked to was the clerk at the front desk. He didn't say much more to me other than hello and here's your room key. He was a young feller, just like you."

That seemed a little strange to me. It sounded like the old timer had found the same door we had used to get out, but there had been no guard posted. Had the old man been the first to get out that way and prompted the placement of a guard to keep anyone else away? And why hadn't he been glommed onto by the manager as everyone else had been who'd ever entered the hotel? It was very confusing. Apparently, Liz was having trouble with his story as well.

"I've been the front clerk at the hotel for a…" she paused for a moment. "…a very long time. I don't recall every seeing you before and there has never been a male front clerk while I've been there."

"Well, now," the old man replied with a wink. "I'm pretty sure I would have remembered someone like you.

Likely I arrived at the hotel and got back out before you arrived."

That would explain it, I thought, but why had that last sentence sounded more like a question to my ear instead of a statement of fact. But if he exited before Liz arrived, that meant he would have been roaming around here for a lot longer than he should have been able to remain alive.

Unless, I thought dismally, that whatever affected time within the hotel also extended down to these caves here. How much more time would pass in the real world before we finally found our way back to it? If we ever found our way back out, that is. I tried to shake off the gloom that had settled on me. We would get out of here; there was simply no other option. I glanced over at Liz and could see she'd had been thinking along the same lines as I had been.

"How long have you been down here?" she asked him.

"I haven't a clue, miss," he replied sadly. "I lost track of time pretty soon and with no daylight coming and going, I could never keep track of the days passing. I hope it hasn't been too long, I'd like to get back to Sara and my gold."

Neither one of us had the heart to tell him exactly how much time had likely passed since he'd come across the Infinity Hotel. By now, I was willing to bet, Sara was bones and dust and his gold long gone too.

"How many of these passages have you checked out so far?" I asked just to change the subject.

"Well, this is your lucky day, folks," he replied, pointing off to a cave entrance off by itself. "I've been through all of them except one, that big one over there against the far wall of the cavern over there. The rest have all ended up leading back here to this here cavern. I'm thinking that has to be the way out of here as there aren't any other openings I haven't yet gone in or come out of."

"That makes sense," I said, feeling a thrill of hope. We wouldn't have to bother with checking all of the caves after all. "There has to be one passage out of here that doesn't loop back."

"Sure has to be," the old miner said with a grin. "I just wish I had tried it first instead of wasting all that time on the others. But I reckon I wouldn't have been here to find you folks if I had, so I reckon that makes all the extra effort worth it."

“Well, it certainly was a good break for us,” I said. “I just hope it doesn’t take too long for us to find the other end of that passage.”

“I second that,” Liz said. “I have had more than enough of this place.”

“I reckon so. Well, if you folks are ready, we might as well get started. The sooner we get going the sooner we find the end of that passage and get out of here once and for all.”

We gathered up our packs and the old man took the lead as we walked over to the passageway out. At least we hoped it was the way out, provided the old man told us the truth and this was the only passage he hadn’t yet explored.

Now, I found myself wondering, why did that thought suddenly pop into my head?

* * * * *

Unlike all of the other corridors we have walked along, a fact the old man confirmed was true in the other corridors he had already explored, this passageway constantly sloped uphill with very few areas where the path flattened out. At no point did it slope downward. Nor were there any sharp-angled turns to be found, with only the occasional gradual turn to the left or right. For the most part, we headed up and in the same direction. No matter where it led us, we definitely weren't heading back toward the cavern.

It also took us a very long time to get wherever it was we were being led to. We suddenly came across a level portion of the passage with a nice outcropping of rock from the wall that would serve nicely as a place to sit and rest.

"We've come at least two or three miles by now," the old man commented after we had all drank some water and eaten some of the jerky. "And by my reckoning, we've been going in pretty much the same direction. We have to be on the right path."

"It even seems a little lighter in here," Liz added and I had to admit that it seemed brighter in here to me as well. Eager to get on with it, I got up and led us onward into the passage, taking Liz by the hand as we started, with the old man bringing up the rear.

Each step we took was another step closer to our freedom from this nightmare. Just the thought seemed to spur us to walk faster and faster until we were almost running along. Then, suddenly, I heard the most wonderful sound I had ever heard in all of my life.

It was the universal sound of traffic, the honking of cars and the chatter of people walking along the street, that one heard in any large city anywhere in the world. All the noises of a large city that got on one's nerves but at this moment, it was the sweetest music to my ears. We rounded a slight curve and there was the end of the passage, a solid rock wall with a simple door set in the middle. The noises of the big city increased as the door came into sight.

"We've found it," I all but shouted with joy. "We found our way out!"

"Thank God," Liz exclaimed. "We're free of this nightmare at last."

We dashed for the door and I grabbed the handle, turned it sharply and threw it open. We stepped into the blinding white light that lay beyond it.

And we quickly came to a sudden, horrified halt when our eyes finally adjusted to the brighter light. We found ourselves standing all alone, right back inside the main lobby of the Infinity Hotel. We stood there, stunned, for only a few seconds before I whirled around to lead us back into the passage.

But the old miner closed the door behind us. As soon as it shut, the door simply disappeared into the solid wall. One moment it was there, the next there was nothing but a blank wall.

"I'm terribly sorry, son," the miner said, even as his body started to change and when his body stopped its metamorphosis, the manager stood there before us. "But I'm afraid you never left the hotel at all, Mr. Childress."

SIXTEEN

All alone in the lobby with Peter and Liz, the manager watched his two escapees closely. Peter had taken a single abortive step toward the now disappearing door before pulling up short. His eyes darted around, desperately looking for an escape route but there was simply none to be found.

The entrance Peter had first used to come into the Infinity was still a solid wall and every other exit in the lobby only led further into the hotel. As it all had been before. Peter's shoulders sagged as he realized that even any access to the park door would likely now be denied to them. There simply wasn't anywhere for them to run to anymore.

Then Peter looked down and saw the tears in his clothing mend, the dirt on his hands and clothing disappear. Peter looked over and saw the same happening to Liz. Within seconds, it was as if they had never been out wandering in the caves at all.

Liz had come to the same realization of their fate a little quicker than Peter and had slumped into a cushioned chair, shaking her head as tears streaked down her face.

"No, no, no," she kept silently mouthing.

The manager chose to simply stand there without saying a word, patiently watching the two come to terms with what had just happened. Patience was what he was best after all. Soon enough, Peter ceased his fruitless search for a non-existent exit and faced the manager.

"Why?" Peter demanded.

"There was no need for the two of you to wander around down there a minute longer," the manager replied. "There are no passages that lead anywhere but back to the cavern or right back here to this lobby. You have to accept that there is no avenue for either of you to leave this hotel and return to the world you left behind when you entered."

"How can you be so certain?" Peter demanded. "There has to be a way out of here. It just isn't possible for there not to be some way to leave."

"All I can tell you is that there is no door you can open," the manager said sadly. "No hole to crawl through, no window to jump out of, not even a roof for you to leap off that will ever get you back to where you came from. There is not even the escape of death here; no one has ever died within these walls and never will. No one has been here longer than I have, Mr. Childress. No one knows this place better than I. Please believe me, I have no wish to see either of you suffer needlessly."

Peter just shook his head but there was little energy in the motion.

"Just let us go," Peter pleaded. "You don't need us here. We're the only ones who know what is really happening here. Why keep us here like this if you care about us at all? Just let us out, let us go."

"I truly wish that I could, Mr. Childress," the manager replied softly. "But that is something that is not within my power to do."

"Then what are we supposed to do?" Peter asked dejectedly. "Just go on knowing the truth about this place and act like nothing is wrong?"

"Nothing so cruel as that," the older man responded. "You simply have to accept staying in the hotel and put the world you once knew out of your mind. In time, you will make the transition without ever realizing it. You and Liz will be together, you can even take over operations here and you both can be very happy. I promise you that it would be a life worth living."

"Alive without living, no change and no end? What kind of life would that be?"

"There are worse fates, Mr. Childress," the manager replied. "Of that I can easily assure you."

It was in Peter to go on fighting, to keep looking for a way out of this hell. Even if the cavern had turned out to be a dead end, there had to be a way out, a way not yet discovered no matter what their jailer said. The manager could easily see that in the set of Peter's shoulders.

But then Peter looked once again at Liz, saw how much this setback had taken out of her. She had been here for far longer than he and who knew how many more years had passed on the outside while he had been trapped inside. Liz's world was long dead and for all Peter knew by now, so was his.

"Liz?" Peter asked, letting her make her own choice. Go on or give in?

"I'm tired, Peter," she said weakly and the manager felt a pang deep within him to see her broken like this. "I'm so very tired."

Peter walked over, knelt next to her and held her close.

"Just let it end, let it be over," she whispered against his chest.

"Okay, Liz," he whispered back softly. "It's going to be okay."

Peter hugged her tight once more before he stood back up and turned to face the manager again.

"So what happens next?" Peter asked, defeat written all across his posture and he would not meet the manager's eyes with his own.

"Nothing at all," the manager replied sadly. "You and Liz will work the front desk and serve our guests. You will be moved into a room together and eventually, you will forget there was ever anywhere else for you to be but right here in the Infinity. It may happen soon, or it might take a little time, but you both will make the transition and never realize the moment when it happens. It will be quite painless, I assure you and you two will be happy together. Why don't you two get some rest first before resuming your duties?"

Peter nodded his head slightly and turned away to reach down to Liz. Even as he started to help her to her feet, their clothes changed to the standard hotel uniform. Neither of them reacted to the change at all. Peter supported Liz as they made their way to the elevators. It was a heartbreaking scene to watch, doubly so because the manager himself had harbored such high hopes for them.

It seems the transition will come quickly for them, the manager thought to himself as he watched them enter the cab. *But what does this mean for me now? We cannot hold many more here. What are the odds that the one we seek has not yet been found?*

The manager slowly walked across the lobby to return to his office, carrying his dark thoughts along with him. Had anyone else been in the lobby area to witness all three of the departures, they might have said the manager looked to be the most downhearted of them all. His head lowered, the manager wouldn't have noticed anyone even if he had encountered them between the lobby and his office. Closing his office door behind him, the manager stopped in the middle of the room and just stood there, lost in thought.

"Damn," he muttered with a heavy sigh. "Damn."

Without his realizing it, the manager's posture slipped into an almost perfect copy of the one Peter had effected just minutes before in the lobby. He reached into his jacket and withdrew his pad, staring blankly at the screen.

"Controller," he called out softly.

"Working."

"How many more can we take on before we reach max capacity?"

"Six."

"Can any adjustments be made to increase maximum capacity?"

"Working," there was a very long pause before the reply came. "An additional fourteen can be added without jeopardizing optimum mission goals."

"If we remove all encoded safety parameters," the manager asked. "What is the maximum amount we can add?"

"Working. Removing safety protocols to absolute lowest acceptable standards would allow an additional eighteen to be uploaded."

Thirty-eight, the manager thought dismally, *only thirty-eight chances left to get it right.*

"Controller," he said aloud. "Resume search protocols. Delete current safety protocols and reset to lowest possible settings."

"Confirmed. Search resumed. Protocols reset."

"Thank you," the manager said. "That will be all for now."

The manager sat down heavily in his chair, dropped his pad onto the desk with a clatter and sat back with a deep sigh. There was only one thing for him to do now and it was the one thing he did best.

He waited. He was getting damnably sick and tired of waiting.

* * * * *

Anthony Wilkerson was a star quarterback in college for the University of Texas and had been drafted by the professional league's Seattle franchise. His rookie season had been lackluster to say the least and he had never once felt like he had fit in with the franchise, its fan base or even with the city itself.

So when the season mercifully ended with the team missing the playoffs, and him still standing on the sidelines with a clipboard in his hands, Wilkerson was more than happy to head back home to Texas. He wondered if his professional playing career would be a lot shorter than he hoped. He really didn't want to play in Canada and the indoor game was not *real* football as far as he was concerned. Fortunately, his mother's insistence on staying all four years at school and getting his degree in botany had ensured that he had a back-up plan in place, just in case football didn't work out.

Although he much preferred running across grass carrying a ball in a numbered uniform than he did walking among the grass wearing a white lab coat and carrying a clipboard, it would pay the bills. It just wouldn't be nearly as much fun or glamorous. Not to mention the hit in his income.

He was having dinner with his parents—his father was stationed at nearby Ft. Hood—at their off base home in Copperas Cove just a few weeks after the league's championship game when his agent called with the best news he'd heard since being drafted.

Seattle had traded him to Dallas, the team he had grown up following as a child and had dreamed of playing for, and he had a legitimate chance to replace Dallas' longtime starting quarterback, who was hinting at retirement after leading the team to the league championship game.

So excited by the news, he barely waited long enough to finish his dinner and give his mother a hug, before dashing out to his car for the one hundred and seventy-mile drive north to Dallas. He wanted to report to the team's headquarters as soon as the doors opened the following morning.

But he had left so quickly that he hadn't bothered to do anything more than pack a quick bag. He hadn't even bothered to get a hotel room reserved in Dallas. He figured he'd find a hotel near his destination when he got there.

Texas had one of the highest maximum speeds in the state, and he more than exceeded that. So just a mere two hours after pulling out of his parent's driveway in Copperas Cove, he pulled up the driveway of the Infinity Hotel. It looked to be located in a very quiet, open area of Dallas.

He handed over the keys to his six-figure sports car and a hundred-dollar bill to the old man who walked out the door to greet him. With his bag slung over his shoulder, Anthony strode quickly through the open doors and headed straight for the front desk. He was used to five-star hotels but this one looked to be easily up in the six-star area.

"Wow," Anthony exclaimed as he stepped up to the desk and placed his ID and credit card on the counter. "This is quite a place y'all have here."

"Thank you," the woman behind the counter, her badge read Liz, said as she looked at his ID, "Mr. Wilkerson. Welcome to the Infinity Hotel."

"Thank you, Liz," Anthony replied, thinking a little flirting with this pretty woman might lead to a little pre-signing celebration later on. "From what I've seen already, I may have to stay around for a few extra days."

"That's what we like to hear," Peter said as he walked up from behind. "Stay as long as you like, Mister…?"

"Peter," Liz said, and the way she said the man's name pretty much ended any thoughts of extra-curricular activities in Anthony's mind. "This is our new guest, Mr. Wilkerson."

Peter must not be much of a football fan, or he hadn't heard the news yet, but he didn't show any hint of recognition that a major sports star was the hotel's new guest. But he noticed that Peter didn't have the slightest hint of any Texan accent either, so Anthony assumed that the man was new to the state.

"Welcome to the Infinity, young man," Peter said with a warm smile, taking a room key card from Liz and offering it to the new arrival. "Just slide this into the reader in the elevator and it will take you right to your floor. As soon as you get settled in, there are plenty of amenities for you to enjoy while you are here."

"Thank you," Anthony said, gathering up his ID and credit card, never noticing that Liz had never picked either of them up. "I'll make sure I check a few of them out."

"Excellent," Liz said as she finished typing in all of the information for the new guest. "Just give us a call if you need anything."

Anthony made his way to his room, 120157, without giving any thought to a one hundred and twentieth floor for a hotel. Nor did it register to him that it hadn't looked anywhere near that tall from the outside. He was still too distracted by his good fortune to register minor details like that.

But he did notice what passed for hotel uniforms for the female staff and completely forgot all about the woman, whatever her name was, down at the desk. He opened the door to his room and immediately wondered if there was a ranking system for hotels that included seven stars. He had never seen a room like this one in his life. He would definitely have to tell his friends back home about this place.

No sooner had he finished getting unpacked than someone knocked on his door. He opened it to find Peter from the front desk on the other side.

"Ah, Mr. Wilkerson," Peter said. "How is your room?"

"Perfect," Anthony answered. "I don't think I've been anywhere better."

"Excellent," Peter replied. "I wanted to let you know about an unlisted amenity we have here for our 'special' guests to enjoy."

Now this was a little more like it, Anthony thought. All top-end places like this had secret rooms set aside for celebrities like himself, the "in" people, to enjoy.

"Sounds promising," Anthony said.

"Very good," Peter replied, holding out a solid black key card for Anthony to take. "If you are ready, I'd be more than happy to show you how to get there."

Of course, he thought, *no use having a secret room if everyone knew how to find it.*

"Let's go," Anthony said, closing the door as he stepped out into the hallway.

Peter led him to the elevators and indicated that Anthony should slip the black card into the reader. As soon as he'd done that, the car headed upward. It kept climbing for some time.

Wow, Anthony thought, *we must be going all the way to the roof or at least almost all the way up to the top.*

He was about to ask just how many floors this place had when the car finally stopped and the doors parted. Peter withdrew the card and gestured for Anthony to step out into the short hallway beyond the doors. Only when he had exited the car did he realize that the hallway was completely empty. There wasn't a door or a single window anywhere in sight.

He spun around to ask this Peter what the hell was going on just in time to see the doors closing shut on the man, who had a strange, sad smile on his face. When the doors closed shut they faded out, leaving Anthony standing in what amounted to a slim white box with nowhere to go.

His entrapment had been so unexpected, so sudden and absolute, that he could do nothing but stand there in shocked silence.

* * * * *

As soon as the doors had closed, Peter had pocketed the black card and punched the button that would take him back down to the second floor where the manager's office resided. He felt a pang of guilt at leaving the unfortunate young man trapped like that, he actually had recognized him almost immediately. The young man had disappeared without a trace some twenty years before Peter's ill-fated trip to Phoenix. Despite a massive search, nothing of him had ever been found aside for his abandoned car, somewhere in Louisiana if Peter recalled correctly. At the time, no one could ever figure out why Wilkerson had headed east for Louisiana when he should have been driving north to Dallas after leaving his parents' home.

Well, at least someone finally knows what really happened to the kid back then, Peter thought wryly as he approached the manager's door. He would have to make sure that he left the black card and a note behind so someone could go up and let the poor kid back out of there. Maybe he should write a note for the kid too. He walked on up to the door and knocked firmly, twice.

"Yes?" the manager called from the other side of the door. "What is it?"

"Excuse me, sir," Peter said as he opened the door. "I hate to disturb you but there seems to be a problem with our new guest."

"Oh?" the manager looked up in surprise, he hadn't been alerted to anything amiss through his usual channels. "Who is it?"

"Anthony Wilkerson, in Room 120157."

The manager scowled as he picked up his pad and scrolled through the readout. He saw the arrival of Wilkerson being recorded by Liz at the front desk and that the young man had made it to his room. After a brief time, he had headed over to enter the elevator and… then vanished! The manager tapped away on his screen furiously, trying to locate Wilkerson but all of his efforts were to no avail.

Could it be?

"He was last spotted in the park, sir," Peter offered. "Apparently, he told another guest about a door that he had found. I went out there and found some footsteps, but there was no sign of him. I wasn't able to open the door to see if he had stepped inside."

The manager pondered the information briefly, unconcerned that Peter appeared to no longer recognize what that door had once meant to him. Even when Peter and Liz had opened that door, they hadn't disappeared from his tracking first. Could this Wilkerson be the one after all? And what did it mean that Peter could not get the door to open now? The guardian had not been reset as there didn't seem to be a need for it. But what if this Wilkerson had figured a way out via the cavern after all? He would have to check it out, just to be certain.

"Come along, Peter," the manager said as he got up from behind his desk. "Let's go see about that door."

The manager had followed Peter out the door so quickly that he neglected to bring his pad with him. His mind raced as he tried to figure out why this new arrival had gone directly to that door and so soon. He wondered, closing the door behind him, if the controller could have found such a qualified candidate so quickly and one that was almost perfectly suited to their needs, that he would make the leap in such a brief time?

There was a quicker, more direct route to that door from the manager's office and they were on the scene quickly. There were indeed two sets of footprints, clearly a man from the size of them and while they were the same size, it was clearly two different pairs of shoes. They led to the door and only one of them had eventually turned away and headed back. This had to have been made by Peter, after he had failed to get the door open.

The manager reached for the knob and twisted it. The door opened toward him easily and the light from the park spilled into the passageway. As he looked in, a thought struck him like a lightning bolt.

There were no footsteps beyond the doorway that led into the cavern!

Suddenly, the manager was struck hard from behind and he tumbled to the hard rock floor. Before he could gather himself, he heard the door slam shut and something big and heavy slam into the door from the other side. He started to get up and try the door, even though he knew it would not open now. Then he thought about hurrying down the corridor to get back to the Infinity's lobby.

Then it hit him, with full force, what had actually just happened to him and the only thing that it could possibly mean. Instead of running, he sat down on a nearby rock and began to laugh in relief.

"Finally," he exclaimed when the laughter finally died off. "Well done, Peter. Very well done indeed."

* * * * *

Peter did not waste a lot of time standing around after he had shoved the manager past the doorway and slammed the door shut behind him. An old tree trunk of great size and weight had been on the brink of crashing over and covering the door and Peter quickly gave it the last little shove it needed to find its final destination. Firmly against the door. Unless the manager had a bulldozer parked somewhere inside that cavern, that door wasn't opening any time soon.

Once the manager was sealed off, Peter knew that he would have precious little time before the man would find his way back to the lobby. He doubted the older man would be too happy with him after this deception. But the risk of that was well worth it, especially if he was right.

He couldn't ask Liz to put herself through this last attempt to break free of this hell in which they had found themselves. He wasn't sure she could take another hope-shattering failure. So he watched as she slowly faded and became another creature of this place. Meanwhile, he had only pretended to go along with the decision to accept their fate and permanently become a part of this madhouse. It had not been an easy façade to pull off and if they did manage to escape, he would apologize to her for the rest of his life for deceiving her as well as the manager.

He had spent his time in his new "position" to carefully scout around the entire hotel, looking for any possible sign of another exit or anything that could be used to facilitate their escape. But no matter where he searched, no such exit could be found.

Then it struck him. There was one place he hadn't been able to thoroughly search, because no one ever went in there alone. The manager's office. There had to be an answer lying hidden somewhere in there. But the problem was how to get in there long enough, without the manager being inside at the time, to do a thorough search. So while Peter plotted a way to draw the manager away, and keep him away long enough, he kept doing his "duties" and appeared for all intents and purposes to be a proper employee.

He was toying with the hotel's key card system when he discovered that he could actually generate brand new rooms by merely entering a previously unused number into the system. After checking to confirm that the recently produced key card in fact actually led to a room, Peter tried creating other rooms aside from the standard guest room and met with success every time. The hotel now had a billiard room and a movie theater for its guests to enjoy.

But what he needed now was a room with a door that could only be opened from the inside if someone was standing inside the room and in possession of the specific access card. In pretty short order, the system generated a black key card and Peter found the room to be exactly what he needed when he traveled up the elevator to check it out. Better yet, the room did not show up anywhere in the hotel's computer system

But there was no way to know if the manager, who surely had an all-access key that would override the lockout, could actually be trapped within that room. Stymied by the lack of knowing for certain, Peter sat back and pondered what his next step would be. When Anthony Wilkerson walked in, the sixth guest to arrive at the Infinity since he and Liz's ill-fated escape attempt, an idea popped into Peter's head.

At any point during their escape, in his guise as the old miner, the manager could have moved them directly back to the lobby. Instead, he had walked along the cavern with them. Which meant there was no shortcut, no quick access card, that would be available to the manager in that cavern. Once in there, it would take him some time to navigate his way back to the lobby.

So Peter had tricked the unfortunate Mr. Wilkerson into the hallway to nowhere, then tricked the manager back into the cavern by creating the two sets of prints leading up to the door for the man to follow and then blocked the door with the old tree trunk. That had been the easy part of the plan. Moving as quickly as he could, Peter returned to the lobby and found Liz behind the counter.

"Liz," he said, grabbing her shoulders and giving her a slight shake. He prayed she wasn't too far gone, as were the other guests, that he would not be able to reach her. "Liz, listen to me, we need to go to the manager's office, quickly."

"Why, Peter?" she replied, puzzled.

"Because it's time for us to leave," Peter answered, looking intently in her eyes and hoping to find some sign of the Liz that had seen through the charade this place was. "I think I found a way for us to get out of here. But we have to hurry."

"Leave…" Her puzzled look remained, but something else grew in there now. "Leave the Infinity? Why…?"

"Liz, remember who you were before you came here?" Peter pleaded, feeling the press of time, as he gently pulled her from behind the counter. "Remember when I first came here. When I went out in the park and found the door, the door you told me about?"

"A door? Yes, there was a door… it led… somewhere." The light in her eyes grew a little.

"Yes," Peter exclaimed as he all but dragged her along with him toward the stairs to get to the manager's office. He'd made the hard choice to leave Charlie behind the last time he thought they had found a way out. He was damned if he would abandon Liz here. "There was a cavern and a lot of caves…"

"And an old man," she interrupted. "Then we wound up back here again and… and…"

"And we told the manager we would stay," Peter finished as they reached the top of the stairs. "But we're not staying, Liz. We are getting out of here."

Liz still looked confused but it was clear what had happened slowly came back to her. At the very least, she would be with him when, or if, he found the way out. That was good enough as far as he was concerned.

They walked into the office, with no sign of the manager to Peter's great relief, and began searching. Not that there was much to search in the room.

"Peter," Liz asked. "What are we looking for?"

Now that was a great question. Peter himself wasn't sure what to look for. A control panel, a hidden door or was it something else? Hopefully, it was something the manager couldn't carry around with him or this little excursion was doomed.

He checked the desk while Liz walked around the walls, feeling for a hidden door or latch. He found nothing, aside from the forgotten pad, which refused to activate for him no matter what he tried. Their search ended without a single clue discovered.

Frustrated, Peter looked around again. Nothing but a chair, a desk and a painting that covered nearly one entire wall and they had looked at every square inch of it all. Nothing.

"Liz," he asked, focusing on that overlarge painting. "Did you check behind that?"

"It's firmly attached to the wall," she answered. "I ran my fingers all around the edge except the top. There aren't any gaps or latches."

Damn, Peter thought as he stared at the painting. Maybe there was a global card after all. But he had watched the manager closely and had never seen him use one.

The painting though, it held his attention for reasons that he couldn't quite put his finger on. It was just a simple painting of the ocean at night with a full moon rising above it. Most paintings he'd seen over similar seascapes tossed in a person standing on a rocky cliff looking out at the sea and the moon while others had an old sailing ship cutting through the waves under the full moon.

Come to think of it, he realized, he'd never seen one so utterly plain like this one. There were no waves, not even a reflection of the moon on the dark water below. Just a perfectly flat, wave-less ocean scene, at night, with a full moon just above the horizon. There was something off about that moon, Peter realized as he stepped closer to it.

"What is it?" Liz asked as she saw what had attracted his attention.

"I'm not sure," Peter replied, raising his right hand toward the shining disk. "It almost looks like the area where the moon has been raised from the rest of the canvas…"

Peter's voice trailed off as he opened his hand and laid his palm directly onto the moon, just over the large crater that dominated the face, and pressed it gently. There was a *snick* and suddenly the whole wall began to swing out toward him. He quickly stepped back out of the way as Liz scampered to his side.

"Peter," she said quietly, as if afraid her speaking would make what they saw vanish. "Is that what I think it is?"

"I think so," Peter replied, a smile of triumph on his face. "I think we just found our way out of this madhouse for sure."

The panel was made up of screens that were mostly dark, but a dimly glowing light came from a hand-sized panel next to a keyboard. This was clearly the on switch and Peter placed his hand on the panel.

"Here goes nothing," he said as his hand made contact.

* * * * *

Still seated on his rock in the cave between the blocked door and the main cavern, the manager noticed the walls of his prison begin to shift, quickly losing cohesion.

The rock underneath him became less solid. A tear trickled down one cheek.

"At last," he said. "It is finally over at last."

Then everything went white.

SEVENTEEN

To tell you the truth, I had no idea at all what to expect next after all of the lights went out in that office. But what did eventually replace the darkness was the very last thing in the world that I had expected to see.

Fog. Lots of billowing clouds of the thick grayish-white variety and they completely surrounded both Liz and I. There couldn't have been more than three feet of visibility and the fog had a cold, damp feel to it. There was even a slight salty smell of the sea that permeated the air. The only trace of color was the ground beneath us.

It was no longer the hard, but even, white tile of the manager's office. We were now standing on green grass and the ground below it felt uneven to me. There was more give to it than I had felt in the park. It felt real, natural, and not a product of someone's creation.

Just as I started to tell Liz that I thought we may have made it to the outside world again, I caught her looking at her arms in amazement. It did not take me too long to figure out what had caught her attention. Because when it hit me too, it had my total attention as well. Neither one of us wore the hotel uniform any longer. Nor were we wearing the clothing we had originally worn when we had first arrived at the Infinity.

Now, enveloped in this thick fog, we were both clothed in simple tunics of white with matching white slacks and boots. It hadn't seemed like more than a second or two had passed since I had shut down the system. Hardly enough time to switch our clothing. Then again it shouldn't have been enough time to transfer us out of the manager's office to… wherever it was we stood right now.

Or had I been wrong all along? Instead of shutting down what had us trapped inside the Infinity, had I instead merely reset it and made it simply alter the nature of the trap?

Yet, what we experienced now had a distinct feeling of being reality. It was most definitely a different vibe than the one that I'd felt within the Infinity. But how different was it? Did different automatically translate into better?

"Peter," Liz asked in a hushed voice as she peered into the fog. "Where are we? Did we make it out?"

I had no idea. Although I heard the sound of other voices, muffled by the fog, and it looked like—at least in areas where the fog was slightly less thick—the vague silhouettes of other people moving about in the fog, calling out to one another. But before I could answer her, someone else beat me to it.

"Oh, I can assure you, Liz, that you are indeed standing outside of the Infinity Hotel."

It was the manager, walking up from behind me. He literally seemed to form out of the fog as I turned around. I imagine that the look of shock and fear that I saw on Liz's face was a match for my own. I had hoped the manager was a construct of the trap and not a real flesh and blood creature.

Yet here he was in the flesh, his feet striking the ground hard enough to generate the sound of footsteps. His appearance was unchanged with the exception that he too wore the same all-white outfit that we were. He also wore what struck me as one of the most genuine smiles I had ever seen on anyone else's face in my entire life.

"Congratulations, Peter," the manager said, grasping my hand and shaking it up and down while I just stood there dumbly. "You discovered the pathway out."

"Did I?" I asked, looking around at the fog that remained wrapped around us.

“Oh indeed yes,” he replied. “I assure you. You are outside, under the wide open sky with terra forma beneath your feet. See for yourself.”

“And how am I supposed to do that with all of this fog in the way?”

“Easily. You can dispatch this mist the very same way that you dispatched the controller in my office a few moments ago.”

“I had a control pad to place my hand on back there,” I replied as I raised my hands in the air and started to move them apart. “What am I supposed to do out here? Just wave… it… awa…”

My voice trailed off as, no sooner had I spread my hands a couple of feet apart from each other, the fog just evaporated until not a trace of it was left behind.

“Yes, Peter,” the manager said gently. “That is exactly what you are supposed to do.”

“Peter,” Liz said, wonder in her voice. “How did you do that?”

Damned if I knew how I had managed that trick, to be perfectly honest, nor was I devoting a whole lot of thought to solving the mystery either. My full attention was on what I was now seeing.

We stood on top of a high hill in the light of a full moon. Maybe a thousand feet or so below us was a beautiful bay, dozens of miles in length with the light of that moon reflecting off its waves, separated from a vast ocean only by a long thin peninsula. The bay opened to the ocean via a slight waterway of no more than a mile in width. All around the bay, the hills were covered in green grass and sandy beaches lined the bay and the ocean shoreline of the peninsula. Waves gently crashed along the shorelines.

It all seemed somewhat familiar to me, even though I had never visited such a place that was so completely unmarked by the type of construction one would see being done by human beings in such a setting. I couldn't even detect any signs of the wildlife that must surely call this place home.

The only signs of life were gathered around our little hillside. Thousands upon thousands of people, of every race and gender, all dressed in the same white outfits, all looking around with the same sense of wonder and confusion.

How had we gotten here? What in the hell was going on? You could see it in every expression within view.

I glanced over at Liz; she had been looking at the incredible scene below. But then she peered up toward the brilliantly shining moon and I followed her gaze upward. Like the bay below, the moon above looked familiar. But it wasn't exactly the same moon that I remembered from before my arrival at the Infinity. The face looked similar, but it was scarred terribly. Cracks and fault lines now gashed the dark craters and dusty white plains.

"I don't understand," Liz said, her voice trembling as a new fear came to mind. "Are we on Earth? Have we been taken somewhere else?"

She had been addressing the manager. The others below had noticed us and made their way up toward us, seeking their own answers to the same questions. But the manager said nothing. He just stood there and looked at me, that same smile on his face that was suddenly becoming very annoying.

"Peter has all of the answers you seek, Liz," he said after a few moments. "He just needs some time to sort it all out."

I opened my mouth to tell him I had no more idea of what was going on here than the next guy when it suddenly shut right back up again. Because right at that moment, it was like someone had opened the flood gates in my mind. I suddenly felt that I was drowning in information.

"Peter!" Liz exclaimed and rushed to my side as my knees buckled. The manager took my other arm.

"He will be all right, my dear," the manager said as he helped keep me upright. "He is dealing with a rather sizeable amount of new information. He just needs to make some sense of it."

Those closest to us had gathered around and the manager turned to address them.

"Perhaps I can fill you all in on my part of the story of the Infinity while we give Peter a moment," the manager said. "First, let me assure you all that you are still on Earth and you are all very much alive. That is the simple truth. The rest of my story, and yours, is a bit more complicated than that, I am afraid to say."

EIGHTEEN

The manager paused for a moment and looked over all of these people whose fate he had taken into his hands. Even now, with a favorable outcome finally secured, one he had almost forsaken all hope of attaining, he was not sure they would understand all that had happened. Nor could he be certain they would approve of what he had done.

He wouldn't even for a second dare to hope for their forgiveness.

But they all deserved to hear him say these words, no matter how difficult they were to speak aloud. So, after taking a deep breath, he began to tell them his story.

"You have all known me as the manager of the Infinity Hotel," he began, letting go of his hold on Peter's arm so he could walk among the others. "But before I took on that title, I was called 'Commander.' Unlike all of you here today, your planet Earth is not my home world.

"My planet orbits a star that your astronomers never discovered," he continued. "Over time, we became explorers of space. We encountered other space-faring races and planets with life that had not yet evolved to the point of understanding there was so much more to the universe than their own world. Occasionally, we encountered species just beginning their journey into space. They were not yet ready to know of our existence, so we watched them and waited for the day when they were ready for us to introduce ourselves. Your planet was one of those.

"My very last command was a mission to the very heart of our shared galaxy. It was to be my last assignment and I wanted to visit your world one final time before my retirement, as I doubted I would live to see the day when our two worlds met."

He paused in recounting his story and stared down at the ground for a few long moments. When he looked back up, everyone could see the great pain that resided in his eyes.

"So we altered our original mission plan," he continued. "Solely so that I could pay one last visit to your world and show those in my command what wonders lay in store for them as they ventured out into the cosmos. The course change was routine and it should have deposited up just behind your moon up there. We would observe your world unseen from there, as we had done so many times over the centuries, and then move on.

"But something went terribly wrong," he continued. "Instead of an orbit just beyond the moon, our ships exited hyperspace well within the atmosphere of your planet. The energy released by our arrival was devastating to your world."

A collection of gasps and exclamations of horror at the thought wove its way through the listeners. There was a fair amount of anger out there too. They had every right to that emotion, the fleet commander thought to himself.

"We quickly passed through and re-entered space," he resumed when the initial reactions died down. "But our passage literally set your atmosphere ablaze. What the shockwave didn't destroy, the searing wave of fire finished off. The stress of our passage triggered every fault line and every volcano on the planet, ripping asunder the crust and allowing molten lava to pour out onto the surface. Nothing survived.

"It is of little consolation to me," he added sadly. "That all of those poor people, all of the living creatures that called your world home, didn't suffer long, if at all. The entire process of turning a living world into a desolate rock began and ended in just minutes.

"We sat out there in space, shocked by what had happened, shamed by our role in it and every one of us wondering if we could ever possibly atone for it. I called together the commanders of all of the ships in my fleet, hoping against all hope to find a solution, find some way to fix what we had done.

"But I will tell you truthfully, when I walked into that room where they waited for me, I knew in my heart that I did not have any hope lying anywhere within me at all."

NINETEEN

No conversation occurred in the room where the seven commanders had gathered. They were all still in too much of a state of shock to say anything. They had each entered the room after their shuttles had docked, walked to an empty chair around the center table and taken their seat without a word of greeting.

No attempts at gallows humor, no attempts to lighten the mood, no recriminations, no explanations. Nothing but stunned silence at what they had seen, what they'd had a hand in causing.

When the commander of the fleet, a man they all respected and admired, a man they had all aspired to become when they were younger and he was already a legend of their home world's space exploration, entered the room, they all looked to him. The silence held as, one by one, they realized that he had no easy solution, no words of comfort to banish the gloom that hung over them all.

"I have never heard of a similar situation occurring before," one commander said, finally piercing the uncomfortable silence. "A star transitioning into a black hole just as a vessel passed near enough for the additional gravitational pull to affect the flight path even slightly. The implications of this to all of our accepted theories is mind boggling. I suspect there will be years of study into the phenom…"

His voice slowly trailed off, merging with the silence, as he realized how meaningless any scientific advancement was in the face of the horror that lay outside the hull of this ship. The fleet's commander did not fault the man, who had been a prime navigator for years before moving up to take his own command. It was easier to focus on the mundane than to contemplate something on the scale of having obliterated an entire living world.

"There must be something we can do," the young commander seated closest to the fleet commander said. She had been the youngest ever to rise to the level of ship commander and this was her first intra-system voyage. She had served on his ship prior to attaining her command. "We know how to travel through time. Surely any restrictions against it can be lifted in a situation like this."

"Kaa'len's Paradox," answered the commander at the far end of the table, not unkindly. The man was nearly as old as the fleet commander and would take over if his predecessor became incapacitated. The two men were also life-long friends. "We cannot attempt to undo what has already occurred, especially involving an event of this magnitude. We would put such a stress on the space/time continuum that we would likely destroy this entire solar system should we even survive the time jump should we make the attempt.

"Likely," he continued. "We might even do such damage as to impact a massive area of space even beyond this system. It could even impact the entire galaxy, perhaps the whole of the universe itself. No, as much as I would gladly sacrifice my own ship and crew if it would prevent this tragedy, that path is closed to us."

"He is correct," the fleet commander agreed, lightly placing a hand on the young commander's shoulder, a slight nod thanking her for trying to find some way to help. "We would do even more damage than we've already done."

"So we do nothing," the commander seated to his old friend's left asked, a note of bitterness creeping into his tone. "We just slink back to our home world, report our shame to the Council of Elders and hope we are not all transferred to command of garbage barge runs to the outer worlds, or perhaps even exiled?"

"No," the fleet commander replied firmly. "The decision to change course was mine and mine alone, as is all of the blame for this disaster. "You all will proceed," the fleet commander continued with a nod in his old friend's direction, "and under the command of the new fleet commander, to our original destination. The mission is too important to abandon, no matter what has happened here. At least some good can still come out of all of this. I will take my ship back to our home world and report what has happened and why to the Council."

As one, all seven commanders began to rise from their seats to protest. Their commander waved them back down.

"This is not subject to debate," he said firmly. "I will return and face the judgment of the Elders and accept whatever they decree my fate to be without question. My guilt is also beyond question. But if there is to be any salvation for the legacy of my career, it lies with all of you, who have served with me so well and for so long, to go on and complete this mission. Will you all do this one last thing for me?"

"Aye." Somberly, and slowly, the word made its way around the table and then the room fell back into the dark silence that had reigned just moments before.

“Just a few seconds of time,” the former navigator said softly, still focusing on the trigger of the tragedy so as to avoid thinking of the terrible outcome. “Either a second or so, earlier or later, either way and we miss the planet by millions of miles. It was just a small matter of time.”

The remark caught everyone else in the room. But while seven minds thought about how such a brief span meant the difference between a living world and billions of dead sentient beings, along with billions of more dead among the lower forms of life, one mind tracked along a much different path.

The fleet commander had begun to pace around the outer walls of the room, considering his last orders to his fleet and then later on to his own crew aboard his flag ship. But the words “small matter of time” had ignited a thought. It might have been one borne of desperation and madness, but a thought it was and it was better than anything else he had to hold on to at this moment.

“What is it?” his old friend asked, seeing the look on his face when he came to a sudden halt.

“A small matter of time,” the fleet commander whispered softly to himself, though the sound of his voice easily carried to his seven subordinates.

"Yes, that was what he said. What is your thought, old friend?"

"We cannot travel back in time and warn ourselves against the course change," he replied. "We know this cannot be done."

"That is correct."

"We cannot prevent this world from being destroyed. But what if we instead save as many of its inhabitants as we can?"

"How many could we save, assuming we survived the jump back?" his old friend asked, the other six commanders abstaining from the conversation. They had chosen to defer to the judgment of these two widely respected veterans. "How would we determine who to save and who to leave behind? Where would we take them where they could have any hope of survival? How long would they last as a species with the limited numbers we could carry on each ship? Assuming they avoid catastrophic losses at some point, could they even reproduce fast enough to sustain their species? Could they even survive the shock of knowing their planet's fate and being uprooted to a new world by an alien species they never even knew existed?"

"Those are all valid questions," the fleet commander agreed solemnly. "But you misunderstand my intentions. I do not propose that we transplant them to a new world."

"Then where are you planning on taking them?"

"Nowhere at all. I plan to resettle them on their own home world."

"But it is nothing but a charred rock in space with no water, no air, no way to sustain life."

"That is correct. That is exactly what it is. At this time."

"Madness," exclaimed his friend, bolting out of his seat as he suddenly realized what his commander proposed. "Even if enough material were deposited on the surface from meteor impacts and even if by some miracle an atmosphere were to eventually reform down there, do you have any idea how long that process would take?"

"Oh, I imagine almost as long as it took the first time around," the fleet commander replied. "But with a little help, I suspect that it would only take a few hundred cycles of this planet around its star to get it accomplished.

"There is enough of the needed minerals and ice locked into the asteroids and comets that litter this system to restore this planet to its former self—or at least as close as possible—and all that is needed is for them to be pushed along on courses to have them strike the surface below. We can construct orbiting generators to form a barrier that will open to allow an incoming object to pass through while trapping the debris, water and carbon dioxide until an atmosphere can reform.

"Once that happens, the surface can be seeded with plants and trees to lay the ground work for a viable ecosystem," he continued. "Finally, animal life and those humans we can save will be brought forward. We will choose those individuals from the past whose disappearance would not be of such an impact on the planet's timeline as to overstress local space and time and create a catastrophic fracture."

A stunned silence fell over the room as they all considered the magnitude of what was being proposed. Finally, the young ship commander—who had first proposed going back and undoing the course change—broke the silence.

"What do you mean by 'a little help?'"

"Four of the ships will proceed out to the asteroid belt that lies between the red planet and the gas giant," he replied. "They will survey the field for the best candidates to replenish the world below, tag them and prepare courses for those targets to travel inward to strike the surface. They not only will provide the needed new material, the strikes will also help push the planet back to its original distance from its star. It seems our arrival managed to nudge it a few million miles closer to the star as well as increased the distance between it and its moon. This also will need to be factored in to bring it back into place so that it can resume its work creating tides for the new oceans.

"Once they have completed that survey, they will move out to the edge of the solar system and do the same for the asteroids and comets that lay out there. We will not only need bodies rich in minerals, metals and water, but we must also make certain that they are not large enough to further fracture the surface so as to undo all of our work. It will not be an easy task to complete."

"And the other half of the fleet?"

"Three ships will work on gathering up whatever material remains in orbit around the planet. We will need to construct the field generators that will serve as the barrier until the atmosphere is rebuilt. We will also need to salvage whatever communications satellites we can locate. They will be needed to track incoming bodies and coordinate with the generators to allow them to pass while deflecting away anything deemed too large and a danger to our designs.

"The flag ship will coordinate between the two groups and do whatever we can to help out when and where needed."

"And then?"

"When we are ready, I will transfer my crew to the other seven ships," the fleet commander said quietly. "Once they are aboard, the fleet will move out to the tagged bodies and use the force tractors to send each one inward. Once all of the targets have been sent on their way from the belt, the fleet will move out to the next field and do the same with all of the targets there.

"Once they have all been sent inward, the fleet will them resume its course to the galactic center and complete its original mission under the command of its new fleet commander. It will then return to our home world and then, and only then, will it report on all that has happened here."

"And where will you be, sir?" the young woman asked.

"Once all of the targets are confirmed to be inbound, and on course, I will take my ship down to the surface and find a secure place to ride out what is sure to be a very long storm. The debris from all of the impacts should do a very good job of burying the ship and the shields should protect the ship from any damage. The monitors in orbit can inform the ship of any potential for direct impact and action can be taken to prevent that from happening.

"Once the bombardment ends, and it is confirmed that there has been enough material delivered to properly terraform the surface, I will begin the process of locating potential targets for rescue."

"How many do you think you can bring forward?"

"Perhaps as many as one hundred thousand and possibly a little more. But I estimate no more than one hundred and fifty thousand humans. The animals and plant life will be easier to store and will take up much less room."

"I am as versed in this method of time travel as you are, my friend," the heir apparent interjected. "You are making this part of your plan sound far easier than it will be. You are going to open a bubble in time and step through it to a place where time does not exist."

"Yes. It is the only way. The ship must be in contact with the planet when the bubble is opened. That is the only way for myself and the ship to exist in every moment of the planet's history simultaneously so we can search for those that we can bring forward, along with all of the animal and plant life we will need to succeed."

"But it will take centuries for the terraforming to take hold and be ready for life, if it even works at all," the young woman said, her voice pained as she considered what that would mean for her commander. "To be trapped in nothingness for so long…"

"Is a small price to pay for what I have caused to occur here."

"And if something goes wrong," another commander spoke up for the first time. "You could be trapped in that bubble for eternity. Worse still, you might never become aware of the fact that you will never get back out. A living death without ever dying."

The fleet commander said nothing in reply. He was all too aware of that possible outcome.

"And the reason why no report is to be sent back," his old friend said. "Is that so much time will have passed before our return home that by the time they become aware of what you have done, it will be too late for them to reverse it."

"At least let some of us stay with you," the young woman implored. "You do not need to do this alone."

"The blame for this is mine alone, as will be the punishment. You would all do me a better service, and a greater honor, by completing our mission and returning home safely to your families. When my work here is done, if it ever is, only then will I return home."

The meeting adjourned as six of the commanders quietly exited to return to their ships to prepare for the task at hand. Only the fleet commander and his soon-to-be successor remained behind.

"Even if you succeed in every other aspect of this, even if you should get as many as one hundred and fifty thousand on board and transit them to a planet that can support life, there is only one way you can ensure they can reproduce enough to survive."

"Yes," the fleet commander confirmed. "The only way to do this is by discovering the genetic flaw in their DNA that blocks their cells from regenerating perfectly. By doing that, I will extend their lifespans and breeding windows. It is the only way to ensure they can produce enough offspring to maintain viability."

"You will be condemned by our Elders and all of our people back at our home world. No matter the motivation, they will never accept what you plan to do here."

"I would rather be condemned," the fleet commander replied. "Than be eternally damned. If I just fly away from this horror without at least trying to make it right, that will be the fate that awaits me."

Nothing more was said for a very long minute as both commanders considered the fate that they could not avoid, even if they had wanted to try.

"Then let us get to work," the successor said finally. "And when I bring the fleet back home, I will do all I can to convince them that there was nothing else that we could have done here. Perhaps they will find it within themselves to be understanding, even if they are unable to be merciful."

"I cannot ask for anything more than that, old friend."

* * * * *

The new fleet commander took half of the fleet out on the survey runs, meticulously selecting the tumbling bodies that carried the necessary materials for what they hoped to accomplish. Working out the trajectories on how to nudge them to their final destination at the precise speeds and angles needed, to not only rebuild the planet but move it back into its former orbital position related to its moon and parent star, took nearly every bit of computer processing that the four ships combined.

The other three ships had embarked on their scavenger hunt, locating two satellites the humans had placed in orbit around their sun and re-tasked them both to track instead the incoming barrage and pass along their information to the eight shield generators they had crafted to serve as a temporary barrier to establish the outer edge of the planet's soon-to-arrive atmosphere.

The planet's lone moon, which now took about ten percent longer to orbit the planet than it had before the incident, completed four full orbits before the seven ships had completed their tasks. The former fleet commander had spent his time preparing his ship for its monumental task while his crew had worked on coordinating the efforts of the other two groups, making sure no step was overlooked.

When the time came and there was nothing more for the other seven ships to do but send the target asteroids and comets on their way, the commander met with his crew for the final time. Standing in the shuttle bay where three transports waited to take them to their new homes, the crew stood at solemn attention.

"You have all made me very proud to serve you as your commander," he said. "And never more so than in how you have all carried out your duties on this very mission. Thank you, for all that you have done.

"Now, I send you to your new assignments and not with a heavy heart in the slightest. I bid you all a safe journey, filled with wonder and discovery and a safe return to our home world to your families. You are dismissed."

As one, the crew snapped to hard attention and saluted their commanding officer one final time. He returned their salute and held it until they had all boarded the shuttles and sealed the hatches. He retreated from the bay to the control console and opened the bay doors, closing them again once the last of the shuttles had departed.

"Controller," he called out after the bay doors had been closed and sealed.

"Working."

"Confirm comlink with the orbiting satellites please."

"Working. Link confirmed."

"Confirm landing area on the planet surface below."

"Landing location confirmed. Coordinates uploaded to satellites and to the fleet."

"Very well. Take us down. I will be in the engine room."

"Confirmed. Beginning deorbit maneuver now."

As its lone occupant made his way through its inner corridors toward its very heart, the sleek black ship fired its maneuvering thrusters and glided downward toward its intended destination. The top of a small mountain, that had once been a small hill overlooking a great bay near a vast ocean less than a planetary year before, had suffered a slight shearing off of its top fifty meters of soil. The flattened area was a perfect place for the ship to roost as the barrage above brought its bounty. The settling debris would cover the ship, literally burying it alive under a twenty-meter-deep layer of new dirt and loose rocks.

If the attempt failed, the ship would remain buried so that, millennia later should life eventually retake its hold on the planet through natural evolution, no one would ever likely find it. He didn't dwell on the possibility that he could fail in his final mission, nor on the likelihood that if he did fail he would likely never know it, trapped in a pocket of endless non-time and forever waiting for a release that would never come. Even if he were to do so, he would not alter his present course. He had no other choice but press forward and let fate make its decision.

He strode into the engine compartment and entered commands, holding off on implementing them until his ship was securely anchored to its new nest. The trip down was so smooth, with no atmosphere to disrupt its passage, that he could not "feel" his ship moving.

Only when he felt the soft thud of the landing legs making contact with the surface, accompanied a few seconds later by the controller's confirmation that they were down and anchored did he enter to commands to get the next phase started.

The engines, no longer needed to power the ship in hyperspace, were now tasked to power the time distortion generator the commander had personally constructed while the other ships had been hard at work on their own respective tasks.

Scientists on his home world had long ago discovered the way to distort space and time in such a way that travel to the past and a safe return was easily accomplished. There had been a handful of such trips, very short and carefully monitored, and they had discovered that not only could they go back in time, but they could also go back to any specific location in time, even if the trip's point of origin was thousands of miles away, as well.

The last time the device was used, they had discovered that the field could be generated in such a way that an indefinite bubble could be opened and a traveler within the bubble could travel to multiple locations in multiple times without having to reset the device. The only limitation was the location had to be somewhere on the same planet where the device was located.

They had hoped to use the technology to replace hyperspace travel, but that had not worked out. After a half dozen trips, the Science Council had taken up the problem of paradox in time travel. So far, none of the six trips had created any problems.

But the potential for disaster, especially in the wrong hands, had decided the matter. The Council, led by Kaa'len, had banned any further use of the technology for traveling in time. But the knowledge, once learned, could not be erased.

The fleet commander had come up the ranks as a scientist and at heart he was always a scientist first and a commander second. He was well versed in the theory behind it and had even continued trying to find a way to use the technology to improve traveling through the void. He had understood and even agreed with the Council's concern with the perils of traveling in the past.

Just as he knew those concerns had no bearing on the situation he was in now.

"Commander," the controller called out just as he finished his adjustments on the device. "The fleet reports that all targets are confirmed to be on course. They are ready to proceed with the mission as planned."

"Our status?"

"The ship is completely shielded and firmly anchored," the controller responded. "All onboard systems at full function."

"Then signal the fleet to get underway," the commander ordered. "Stand by to initiate the bubble."

"Acknowledged."

A little over two hundred million miles away, the last of the seven sister ships finished their work. Once they arrived at a tagged asteroid, their controller calculated the amount of force needed to send the object on the correct course and speed to miss the other three inner planets, avoid colliding with another inbound object and strike the third planet in the system at the correct time and place.

Once the object was sent on its way with a nudge from a tractor, the ship would move on to the next target and repeat the process. Once the belt had been cleared of all of the tagged asteroids, the ships had moved on out to the edge of the system and started the process all over again. Back on the now landed ship, its controller would continue to monitor every target's progress and faithfully reported to its lone occupant.

"Commander, our orbital monitors confirm that all targets are inbound and on course."

"Thank you," he replied simply as he moved to the center of the room. "Initiate the bubble. It is time for us to get started on our part."

"Acknowledged. Bubble initiation… now."

In the middle of the room, a small ball of shimmering light appeared and began to enlarge. Pulsing yellow-white, the little orb quickly expanded out to the size of a sphere about the size of a human head. Then, with a final flashing pulse of brilliant white, it snapped into its full size, a sphere completely englobing the entire ship.

"Bubble initiation is complete, Commander. The bubble is stable. All systems remain at full function."

The fleet commander released a small sigh of relief. *So far, so good.* He was now literally nowhere, and yet at the same time everywhere, in space in time on this planet. Because they existed in every moment simultaneously, the controller could continue to monitor the progress of the terraforming while at the same time search for those they could bring forward.

For now, all the commander could do was continue to prepare for their arrival, listen to the updates and hope in the end that it would all work the way he had planned. They would not actually take on passengers until they had confirmation that a livable world awaited them.

* * * * *

Out at the edge of the system, after months of sending targets inward, the final tagged object that had been sent on its way had been a comet, full of frozen water, that had faithfully lit up the skies of the planet it was now destined to become a part of every seventy-eight years or so. This would be its last trip sunward. The species that had lived on the planet had once believed it to be a harbinger of evil to come. This time it would hopefully be a much better omen.

The target planet had completed an entire orbit around its sun since its destruction just as this last object was sent on its way to impact. Once they had confirmed that the hundreds of targets were indeed still on course, a few of the closer ones had already found their mark while one had missed, the fleet commander sent a final message of farewell to his old friend and then ordered his fleet to continue on to their original destination.

* * * * *

"Commander, the fleet reports the final object is underway and they are departing as ordered."

"Thank you," the former fleet commander responded. The benefit of being inside the bubble was that it seemed they had just opened it up, yet clearly a fair amount of time had already passed outside. Perhaps the waiting would not be so bad after all. "As soon as the last object has impacted, let me know."

"Acknowledged. Commander, the new fleet commander has attached a private message for you."

"Put it on display."

The old fleet commander read the brief message and smiled sadly.

"I would have done the same," it began. "Had it been I in your place instead. Know that no matter what our historians write about you in the future, we, your fleet, your comrades, know that you have acted with honor and did what was truly right. May fate find a way to properly reward you, my old friend."

* * * * *

Outside, the planet completed two more circuits around its parent star before the final object impacted the surface. Over ninety-five percent of the objects succeeded in finding their target, they had factored in miscalculations and unforeseen circumstances and could live with a ninety percent success rate. The ship had easily survived the barrage, the nearest impactor had been over three hundred miles away, and was now buried under a full twenty meters of debris.

Inside, it seemed like less than a few minutes had passed before the controller made its final report.

"Commander, the final object has struck. We are well within the needed parameters to proceed."

"Very good. That is very good news indeed. Do we have our first targets located?"

"Affirmative."

"Then initiate the Infinity directive."

TWENTY

We all listened in stunned silence as the manager, the fleet commander, whatever his name was, finished his account of the days, months and years that followed the destruction of our world.

"The generators in orbit kept the debris and materials from the impacts contained," the old man continued. "But it still took years for it all to settle back down onto the surface and for all of the ice to melt and form into the oceans, lakes and rivers. Ice formed again at the new poles. We had placed generators in the land to pump out carbon dioxide to help build up the atmosphere quicker. It took decades of real time before all of the generators, above and below, could finally be shut down.

"But when they had finished their work, there was finally a livable world here again. Trees, plants and seedlings of every species to have ever grown here were collected and transplanted over every land mass that lay above the waters. It was not a perfect replica of what had been before, but it was very close and it would more than suffice.

"Then, all that remained was to locate as many of you as we could hold, as well as all of the various lower life forms from the smallest insect to the large marine mammals. I met you, for the very first time, as the old doorman to lead you into the time bubble. It was the only time I existed in the real world. And then all I had to do was wait for you to arrive, Peter."

"Why him?" someone in the crowd called out.

"Because I knew even by making the DNA alterations in all of you, giving you a much longer lifespan," he replied. "That even that might still not be enough to guarantee your survival. There was one more thing I could do, and only that one thing, that would ensure this had all not been for nothing."

"The one thing being what your leaders back home would condemn you for?" I interrupted.

"Indeed," he confirmed. "I knew I would need to 'enhance,' for lack of a better term, one of you. I needed to give one of you the ability to not only control the environment around you, but to alter it completely as would be needed. It was not an ability to be bestowed lightly and only someone who met a very specific criteria could be entrusted with it.

"We had come close a few times," he continued. "Even before you arrived, Liz, and a couple of times after, I was almost certain that we had finally found our candidate. But none of them proved themselves worthy. And then Peter arrived. I must admit I had begun to give up hope by then. And no sooner did I dare to hope, I feared that we had failed again when you yielded so easily in the lobby after the caves. You have no idea how relieved I was when you shoved me through the door and blocked it closed behind me. I knew at that moment that it would be all right."

"This ability," I asked. "What exactly is it?"

"You know the answer, Peter," he answered. "You've already used it and more than once at that."

"When?"

"When you cleared the fog away just a few minutes ago. The first time was back in my 'office' when you actually shut down the time bubble, transferring all of these people back to the outside world. You now have the ability to alter existing matter at the molecular level. The fog cleared away because you converted all of the hydrogen atoms within it into oxygen. Back in the office, the act of placing your hand on the pad began the process, controlled by you, to not only collapse the bubble, but to physically move everyone outside of the ship as it collapsed."

"You're saying I did all of that just by thinking it?" And I admit I felt a cold chill run up my spine.

"Well, that's a simplified way to describe the process, but yes. Is there a problem?"

"Hell yes, there's a problem," I exclaimed. "One person with that kind of power scares the hell out of me, especially when I am that person. How do you know I won't abuse it? How do you know I won't do something terrible, even by accident, with an errant thought?"

"That isn't quite how it works," he said, a smile breaking out on his face. "And you have no idea how relieved I am to hear you ask those questions as your initial reaction."

"Why?"

"Because, Peter," he replied. "It means you are truly the right choice for this gift. That your concern would be the potential of misuse ensures that you will never misuse it. Besides, that is what Elizabeth is here for. She is your anchor, to keep you grounded so that you will never do harm in that way. She has always been the key to discovering who would be entrusted with this responsibility for she would be the one who could keep that person balanced. I think you would agree with that sentiment, Peter."

Well, I certainly couldn't disagree with it. But I was not convinced that whatever had been done to me was that great of an idea. The old line about absolute power corrupting kept ringing in my head. An angry thought could become disaster.

"You will need this ability, especially now at the beginning," he continued, taking my silence as agreement. "There is much that still needs to be built here, and quickly. You know all you need to know about how many people are here, what their needs are and how best to employ them. All of that information was transferred into you the moment you placed your hand on the pad."

It was all true, every word he said, as I could suddenly confirm. Just the thought of asking triggered the needed information as I discovered with my first question: How many of us were there? The answer, not only in an exact number but also in where they had been gathered from across the Earth caused me to shoot a look at our rescuer.

"Did a little reading of Earth literature over the centuries, did you?" I asked him. "The Bible caught your attention?"

"A little," he replied, his slight smile telling me that he knew what had prompted my response.

There were exactly one hundred and forty-four thousand people gathered around this hill, far more than the mere six thousand he had said were inside the Infinity before. The ship had broken down the planet into twelve regions and collected exactly twelve thousand people from each region. We had become a modern-day twelve tribes of Israel.

With that information came the quick realization that I could put a name and a face to every single member of that vast multitude below. More, I knew all about each of them. What their skills were and what they would want to do in this new world of ours and how that could be meshed with all of the others.

Caught up in the cascade of information, I could see how best to set up our new communities across the globe. We would not put all of our eggs in one basket as it were, we would not be gathered up in this one small area—which I now knew for a fact to have been the San Francisco Bay Area—and pile tall buildings on top of one another, cramming in a large number of people into a small space as our people had done before in the big metropolitan cities in the past.

No, we would create small towns, of no more than four thousand each, roughly forty new towns divided across the globe. With the new awareness, I could see that most of the old continents and land masses were now much as they had been before, with some minor differences. Towns would be placed in North and South America, Europe, Asia and Africa, the numbers equally divided up to ensure that one catastrophe would not take out the entire human race again.

There were several regions that were perfectly suited for growing crops in large enough quantities to feed everyone, on top of any of the produce generated by each town's local growers. Hunger would never trouble humanity again.

We even had a built-in specialist in botany who could oversee that. He might even have enough time to start a new football league if he wanted. I figured that I owed Anthony Wilkerson that much for ruthlessly trapping him in that hallway like that. I made a mental note to look him up later, as I did not see him standing close by, and apologize to him for that. I had a feeling he wouldn't hold it against me under the circumstances.

Nor would energy be an issue for our new world as it had been before. There were no longer any petroleum deposits to drill for, not that there would be a need for them if they had existed.

Recalling some of the Nikola Tesla designs that I had studied back in college, the converters in orbit would be re-tasked to collect energy from the sun and transmit it to surface towers below which would then distribute the energy to the homes and businesses. Perfectly clean, constantly available power. I suspect Tesla wouldn't have minded my borrowing his ideas and he likely would have loved to have seen it in person. I did a quick inventory of our population but Tesla was not there.

And suddenly, just in a blink of an eye, I saw it all in its finished form. It was incredible and all that remained to do was to think the word 'begin' in my mind. The oohs and ahhs from the others drifted up to where I stood as I heard Liz gasp.

Looking down at the bay below, we could see the buildings form, like a child constructing them one Lego brick at a time, the central energy tower rose up from the ground, walkways led to the houses, which lit as the tower began receiving the energy from above. Without actually being there, I knew that across the planet in thirty-nine other locations, a similar process took place.

Within ten minutes, New San Francisco was completed and stood waiting for its residents to arrive. On what had been Treasure Island, between San Francisco and Oakland, walkways appeared, reaching out across the water until they made contact with each shore. The island itself sported two buildings. The smaller one was a home, the larger was a library. Here, as would be the case for each library that also appeared in all of the other cities, was every volume of fiction and non-fiction ever written, every sheet of music written or recorded, every film, television show, documentary, photograph, newspaper and magazine, every single bit of information collected by the human race. Even lost volumes from ancient times had been recovered and translated. It had all been collected by the ship as it scanned every moment of time and now it was ours to enjoy once again.

The ship had also collected two of each species of animal and insect life, some that had been long extinct at the time of Earth's demise, and preserved them as well. It was a simple matter of cloning from the originals and placing them on the farms and ranches of each city. Those species not needing to be herded, were scattered across the planet where they could best survive and thrive.

"Your ship's name wouldn't happen to be 'Noah's Ark,' would it?" I asked and got a shake of the head along with a soft chuckle back in reply.

"Is that where we are going to live? Which one is our home?"

I heard these questions in several variations, but oddly all in the same language. I didn't need to look at our savior for an explanation. Reducing the cacophony of languages into one basic language made things a lot easier. It seemed like no one language had gained supremacy in the transaction either. There were words from all of the old languages intermixed together and it seemed we all could easily understand it as if it had been our mother tongue all along.

"Friends," I called out as loud as I could, trusting that those who could hear me would pass along what I said. "There is a home for each couple and all will be explained to you when you arrive at them. There is a computer system built into each that will aid and inform you as needed."

"But how do we know which house is ours, do we just pick one?" called out a man who I recognized as being one of the Romans I had encountered in the elevator.

"They will take you there," I answered, looking up in the sky.

For decades, we had been promised flying cars and it had never happened. Until now. A fleet of air cars descended from the eastern sky, each heading as if guided to the two passengers it would transport to their new home. A yellow underbelly with a clear canopy overhead and seating for two and a cargo area, they were shaped like the old AMC Pacers, only with no wheels. Landing struts descended from the underbelly when it came time to land. And they were powered by engines that tapped the flow of energy transmitted from the generators above. These engines also ran silently.

It had taken nearly an entire mountain of material to convert into all of these cars, but they turned out quite well, if I do say so myself. Of course, if there were any Tibetan monks anywhere in this lot of survivors, they weren't likely to be too happy to discover that there was now a huge valley where Mt. Everest used to stand.

The cars landed and called out the names of their new owners, who quickly boarded and sped off to their new homes. Many flew down to the town below, the rest scattered off in every direction. The anger died off, slowly, with the realization that we had all been given a new lease on life. As the explanations that would await them in their new homes filled them in, I suspected the anger would be gone completely. There had been no malice. It had just been a terrible accident.

With the sun still an hour away from casting its first light on the eastern horizon, the last car departed, leaving me, Liz and the manager gathered together while no more than a dozen yards away was Charlie, Carrie and a dozen other people. They walked over to us with confused looks on their faces.

"Hey, Pete," Charlie asked as they got closer. "What about us?"

"You all will be heading to New Zealand," I replied mysteriously.

"Why there?"

"Jurassic Park is still your favorite film, isn't it?"

"Sure."

"Well," I said slowly, drawing out the moment. "We call it Australia now."

"No way!" he exclaimed.

"Yep. It looks like a big salad bowl now with all of the vegetation. But it is filled with every species of dinosaurs and other animals that went extinct. They've been altered to only be herbivores and not be a threat to any other man or beast, but they are all there and in the flesh."

Charlie was geeked out, as I knew he would be, and Carrie was equally thrilled. That was to be expected as they were perfectly compatible with each other. The other twelve in their party each wore beaming smiles. They had been scientists before, specializing in the old, lost creatures of the distant past. They would happily spend an extended lifetime studying living specimens.

"There is a small town set up for you in New Zealand," I explained. "About one thousand residents for farming and other things needed to support a town. You will reside there and the animals will have Australia all to themselves. There's even an inland sea for the amphibians to hang out in."

"Thanks, man," Charlie said, the others adding their gratitude as well, just as seven air cars settled down behind them. "I told you I'd get us where we need to be."

"That you did, Charlie," I replied with a laugh, realizing I wouldn't have to apologize to him for abandoning him on our first escape attempt. "You enjoy yourself over there and I expect to see lots of pictures."

"You bet," he said as he and Carrie walked to their waiting car.

"And Charlie," I called out right before they got in. "Keep your hands off the controls. The last thing you need to do is take another one of your damn shortcuts."

Charlie laughed and waved goodbye. I watched the small group of cars fly out over the ocean to the southwest until they faded from view. And then there was only the three of us left on the hill.

"It would appear my task here is complete," the commander said. "It is time at last for me to return to my home."

"What will they do to you when you get back?" Liz asked.

"I am not certain," he replied. "But I very much doubt that I will be returning to a hero's welcome. Even after so much time has passed, whatever punishment the Council decreed when my fleet returned home and gave their report will likely still be waiting to be enforced. At best, I will likely be exiled to one of the outer moons."

"You could remain here," I said. "You would be welcome among us, I'm pretty certain of that."

"Thank you," he answered sadly. "The offer is more generous than I deserve. But this is not my home world. Even in exile at least I would be close by."

"I understand," I said. "But if you do ever need a place to call home, there will always be a place here for you."

He did not respond, but I could tell he was deeply touched by the offer. Instead, he turned to Liz and placed a hand on each shoulder.

"Take good care of him, Liz," he said. "Live a long and happy life together,"

"You know I will," she replied, drawing him into an embrace. "And, thanks to you, we will do that too."

He pulled back and extended his hand to me.

"Goodbye, Peter," he said. "Thank you for this small bit of redemption. Whatever lies ahead for me, I can face it now, knowing that this world and her children are alive and well again."

He started to turn away to head for his ship, but I would not let go of his hand. Puzzled, he stopped and looked at me.

"You're not sure your ship can make it back, are you?" I asked, uncertain how I even knew that. But by the look on his face, I knew that I had been right. Giving him a stern look, I let go of his hand and walked over to the still open bay door of his ship and placed my hand on the interior wall.

The lighting had been dim, making it hard to see inside, but from the contact with the ship, I could tell it had taken a pounding over the centuries and its power cells were nowhere near capacity. It had taken nearly everything the ship had to pull off the monumental tasks it had been given by its commander.

Well, I thought to myself, that was something that was certainly easily fixed. The ship was buried under a thick layer of rock and dirt. As before, I could see what needed to be repaired, replaced and recharged. In less than two minutes, all of the debris above had been converted to repair damage, restore the hull's integrity and fully power the ship. Now it was ready to fly home and successfully make the journey.

"You should have asked, you know," I scolded him after the task was complete.

"Perhaps," he allowed. "But I didn't want to presume."

"Goodbye," I finally said to him. "Have a safe trip home."

"Farewell," he replied and walked toward the open bay.

"One last thing," I called out suddenly, even as Liz came up and put her hand in mine.

"Yes?" he asked, stopping just at the edge of the bay.

"We won't see each other again, will we?"

"I doubt it, Peter. The Council has likely banned travel here and will extend that ban for a long time to come. I assume you plan on eventually moving out into space?"

"Seems the smart thing to do," I confirmed. "By moving out into the solar system, we avoid losing the human race to a single event again."

"Indeed. But that will take some time before you are ready to venture out, even longer before you reach my world. You might live long enough to see my world, but I won't live long enough to see that day."

"Then can we see what your kind really looks like?" I asked. "I know your true form is not humanoid like ours."

"No, it isn't," he said. "Are you certain you want to see it."

"Yes," both Liz and I answered at the same time.

"Very well," he said as he reached into his pocket and withdrew an old-fashioned silver pocket watch attached by a slender silver chain. He pressed down on the latch release, popping open the cover. He then pressed his thumb on the face of the watch.

His body shimmered and when it had ceased the

human we had known as the manager, the fleet commander, was no longer standing there. In his place was the fleet commander in his true form and it was a very alien form indeed.

It wasn't a little gray man like the old movies used to portray. He was almost reptilian, if reptiles ran around on two legs. His body was covered in scales and nearly all a burnt orange in color with a pale yellow belly. Even standing, he was only all of four feet in length, his hands and feet strikingly similar in appearance and each with four digits, one an opposable thumb. With no noticeable neck, nor a tail, the head was completely hairless.

The head reminded me of a horned frog, spiked at the top with a thick ridge just above the black eyes, which were set off a little to each side. There was a snout of a sort and a mouth that extended forward slightly. His species "spoke" in a series of whistles and clicks that, with this newfound wealth of knowledge stored in my head, I knew I could understand if I heard it. I wasn't so sure I could speak it back however.

The fleet commander stood there for a minute, letting us take it all in, before raising his right forepaw, spreading out the four webbed digits as far as he could, his meaning clear, his final farewell.

Liz and I both returned the gesture then backed away as he disappeared into his ship and the door closed behind him. After a few minutes, the ship silently lifted off the hilltop and flew off into the sky. Just as the sunlight began to peek over the horizon, the ship darted off, out of sight. He was finally on his way home.

"Peter," Liz asked as we turned away. "Where are we going to live? I don't see a place or a car for us."

"The car is on its way," I said. "As for where, our place is just over there."

I pointed off to the west, along the ocean side of the peninsula where we could make out a small outcropping of rock with a sandy beach between it and the waves below. About thirty feet above that beach, a flat area in the rocky area suddenly formed into our house. I heard our car gently settle down behind us even as the last bit of construction was completed below.

"What do you think?" I asked her.

"Perfect, Peter. It's just perfect," she replied.

"Not just yet," I said. "There's one last thing left to fix."

"What? I don't see a thing wrong with it."

"With the house? No," I said, pointing up above the rocks to the bright full moon hanging in the sky above. It had taken quite a few lumps over the centuries and it looked nothing like either of us remembered. "That simply will not do."

Almost as if a giant, invisible eraser were at work, all of the jagged gouges, fault lines and other signs of damaged began to disappear. Soon enough, the moon was its old self of craters and maria once again.

"Now that is perfect," Liz said.

"Let's go home," I said, taking her hand as we headed off to our future.

TWENTY-ONE

As the human race settled in on New Earth, time had lost all of its hold on the species. With the extension of their life span, there was no longer any need to keep track of the passage of time. Things were completed when they were completed. Deadlines were unnecessary. No one was in that big of a rush.

Still, a few people held out and kept track of the passage of the years, just for argument's sake if for no other reason. By consent, the era of humanity was divided into two time periods. The time before the great destruction and the time that began the moment when Peter had led the rescued back out of the ship.

By their reckoning, a millennium and a half had passed since the Earth had been scoured in searing flames and nearly a millennium had passed since the human race had reclaimed their home world.

During that time, so much had occurred. A new form of government had been built. Each town was responsible for its own area and would send one representative to the planetary council whenever the council was called into session, which wasn't very often.

The idea that the individual was superior to a central government, that the individual was not only free to live his or her life as he or she saw fit, but that the individual was also responsible for his or her own actions as well as any consequences that resulted in said actions, had taken firm hold. Crime was non-existent as were want, hunger and all of the other dark things that had plagued mankind through the years before.

Peter's original plan of creating small towns, capping each town's population under five thousand, had also held through the centuries. Nowhere on the planet could one find the crowded, overpopulated megacities that had littered the planet before. The entire planet was habitable, and could easily sustain the small towns. They were spread out across all of the continents, save Australia which had its thriving population of non-human creatures, with plenty of room to live and even more room to continue growing. Even ten centuries after the original one hundred and forty-four thousand had set foot on the planet once again, the Earth's total population remained well under thirty million. On the planet that is.

Peter's concern not to put all of Earth's eggs in one basket had also held. They had all learned that lesson and all too well. In time, a colony was established on the restored moon, they had even found the remains of the Apollo missions and created monuments at each site, the last remnants to the pre-history of New Earth.

Just a century later, Mars had been colonized and terraformed. Ceres, which had remained untouched in the mission to replenish Earth from the asteroid belt, Jupiter's moon, Europa, and the moons of Saturn, Titan and Enceladas, soon followed suit. Forty-four hardy souls had even colonized Pluto, setting up an amusement park on the heart-shaped plain. They called it Planet Disney, claiming no one was around to sue them for copyright infringement so why not?

One man, who had been a writer before the incident, claimed the plain looked more like the animated character that shared the planet's name. He'd also mentioned that calling Pluto a planet was a form of justice too, seeing as how it had been wronged by a group of, as he called them, "really dumb scientists" to begin with.

The human race had quickly reached the edge of its home solar system and they had no intentions of stopping there. Outward they went, visiting Alpha Centauri and discovering that its lone inhabitable planet held the early forms of life that might one day also reach the stars. Knowing all too well from their own experience the hazards of first contact, the system was closed to all traffic and only a very small monitor was left behind on a nearby desolate moon. It would inform the humans of Earth when the time had come, if it ever did, to return to Alpha Centauri and finally say hello.

In the beginning, the human race had kept close to home, searching only its closest neighbors, looking out for other life and mapping out any of the worlds they found that could possibly serve as future homes for humanity. One day, in the still distant future, Earth's sun would die and take its planets with it. Not even Peter's ability could prevent that. Humanity would simply have to move on, finding suitable worlds, free of higher life forms, to move to when that time finally came.

So far, they had not yet run into any of the space-faring races. The one they knew for certain did exist, they weren't quite yet ready to reach out to. So they kept growing, kept colonizing and exploring until they were. Even despite the wealth of knowledge they had been bequeathed, there was still so much more to learn and discover in a seemingly endless universe.

Their shipbuilding improved exponentially with each passing generation. They had discovered a way to traverse from one point in space to another, no matter the distance involved, in transits that lasted from as long as the span of an hour to as brief as the blink of eye.

The new tunnel drive generated a sphere in front of the ship. On the one hemisphere of the sphere was the entry point. On the other side of the sphere was the exit point, determined by the destination coordinates programmed into the drive's engines.

Once the sphere had stabilized, the ship entered the sphere and traversed along a wormhole like tunnel within that sphere. Once at the end of the tunnel, the ship exited at its target destination. So far, the longest transit time had been fifty-eight minutes to get to Procyon, over eleven light years distant from Earth.

When the millennial of New Earth neared, only one course of action was really considered. The time had finally come to visit the home world that had impacted Earth's destiny so greatly. Wolf 424 was a binary system of red dwarfs and a dozen planets that lay just over fourteen light years away.

Four of those planets revolved within the orbital paths the two stars took as they circled one another. The stresses on those four planets rendered them uninhabitable. How they even remained intact under assault from such forces defied explanation. But of the remaining eight planets, three were in the so-called "Goldilocks" zone that Earth itself resided in around its own star.

The ninth planet in the system, a desert-like planet was the fleet commander's home world and the destination the travelers set their sights on for a new class of ship. But Wolf 424 was not the new ship's final destination by any means. The new vessel would then move on to a more daunting destination: The faraway Andromeda Galaxy.

At over two million light years away from Earth, no one knew how long the transit would take. Theories flew back and forth, including one that had the ship trapped forever inside the sphere. That one hadn't gained much traction but it couldn't be completely discounted either, at least not until after the first attempt was made and the matter was settled once and for all.

But it would be made, that much had been determined, because that was the destiny of the human race. To seek. To find. To learn. And when the question came up as to who would lead the mission to the new galaxy, there were almost as many candidates for the job as there were theories as to its destiny. But when two certain candidates stepped forward, they had immediately disqualified all of the others, not that any of them would have challenged the pair for the job after they had thrown their names in.

For a thousand years now, Peter and Liz had watched over the human race as if each and every one of them had been their own children, of which they themselves had produced an even dozen. None of their children had inherited their father's ability to alter molecular structures, the trait hadn't shown up in anyone else since either, which made Peter suspect that whatever alteration had been done to him had to have been a deliberate operation and one not capable of being genetically produced.

His ability had always made him slightly uncomfortable and he was glad no one else had ever manifested it. There was just too much opportunity for disaster, intended or not, to suit him. In the early years, he'd used the ability to secure and stabilize the towns across the planet. There had been adjustments to make in the power generators and other devices needed to be constructed to help, if not control, then at least to modify the weather so as to prevent loss of life.

Earth was still an active world of volcanoes and earthquakes and the worst of these events required some attention. He could not prevent them, but he could redirect the lava flows and repair the damage from the quakes. No one had ever lost their lives in one of these events; they had developed early warning systems and the limited populations nearby had all but eliminated the chance for anyone to perish in one.

As time went on, Peter found himself using his ability less and less until decades and a couple of centuries had passed by without him using it. While he was more than happy to help save lives when needed, Peter had always firmly declined any attempt made to put him in a position of authority. He would advise and guide, but the reins of power, those he wanted nothing to do with at all.

Liz had been his anchor throughout it all, but she had also thrown herself fully into her family. Their first child had been a daughter and Peter had suggested she be named Audrie, just close enough to Liz's first lost child while still preserving the newborn's own individuality. Four more daughters and seven sons followed. Then had come the grandchildren and the great-grandchildren and all the generations that followed.

Peter had often marveled at how Liz could keep track of each of their names and relationships, especially when the family's numbers reached into the tens of thousands, and he always loudly claimed that he barely could remember which grandchild was which. Liz wasn't fooled at all. Peter knew them all just as well as she did and took as much pride in every single one of them, just as did she.

But in time, it became clear that their progeny, much like the rest of the human race, no longer needed to be shepherded and the mission to Wolf 424 and then to Andromeda was just what they were looking for.

So when Peter let it be known that he and Liz wanted to go out on the flight, no one considered saying no, not even for a moment, especially when their first visit with the Wolfians was concerned.

This time, Peter could not talk his way out of command, no matter how hard he tried. While the final construction on the large ship wrapped up, Peter went about choosing the crew. The ship would also carry a group of colonists and all of the supplies they would need. The two thousand volunteers and their cargo would travel aboard the ship inside the same type of time bubble that the commander had preserved the originally rescued within those fifteen centuries before. When, and if, a suitable world could be found in Andromeda, they would be brought out. If not, they would stay inside and the ship eventually returned to its home galaxy.

It was a gamble, but they were all but certain to find a hospitable world over there, so none of the volunteers were overly concerned.

The ship would be crewed by fifty people, including Peter and Liz, and was made up of engineers, a doctor and two nurses and a host of scientists in different fields to study the new galaxy. A rotating bridge crew of communications and navigators rounded out the roster with Liz serving as the official chronicler of the voyage. Peter quipped that his job was to sit in the command seat and look coolly serious and do little else.

After a year's preparation, the ship was christened with her new name, officially recommended by Liz, and when she left Earth's orbit, her name was painted in large block letters of gold along the lengths of both of her winged-shaped black hull, *Infinity*. She coasted away from the inner planets, to a safe distance where her engine could be brought up to full power to engage the tunnel drive. When the sphere had formed and the coordinates were triple-checked—a lesson learned from the Wolfians' disastrous error that had destroyed Earth—the *Infinity* slipped into the entry point.

Although the overall distance was the greatest they had ever attempted yet, the transit to cover over fourteen light years of space took only twenty minutes of real time. No one had ever figured out why the length of distance traveled did not correlate to the amount of time spent in transit, and the *Infinity* entered the Wolf 424 system precisely on target and less than a day's cruise at normal speed to the ninth planet.

The *Infinity's* unexpected appearance in the system had certainly caught the attention of the planet's ruling council. Alerts sounded across the planet and every ship in orbit powered up in case this new unknown vessel was a threat.

"Planetary defenses have been engaged," the Infinity's control computer announced to the bridge at large.

"Navigation," Peter called out to the young woman, who had celebrated her two hundredth birthday the day before they departed. "Bring us in slowly and park us in a high orbit until we're officially invited down."

"Acknowledged," the navigator confirmed, entering the course and speed corrections on the panel in front of her.

"Communications," Peter said, turning to the rear of the bridge. "Are we on their primary frequencies?"

"Coming online now," the man replied. "The translation program is up and you can begin your message now."

"Thank you," Peter said, pressing down on the transmit panel. He could replicate the clicks and whistles of their language, with some effort, but it was much easier on the vocal chords to let the computer handle it.

"This is the New Earth vessel, *Infinity*," Peter began. "We are on a mission of peaceful exploration. We have come to your world to establish formal contact between our two worlds and to seek out news of one of your commanders who visited our planet fifteen hundred years ago. We are no threat to your world. We seek permission to take orbit around your world and to send down representatives to the surface."

Peter lifted his hand off the panel and nodded to his communications specialist. The man quickly tapped a series of squares on his main panel.

"Message translated and transmitted," he reported. "Standing by for a response."

"Keep repeating it every ten minutes until we hear back from them," Peter ordered. "It may take them a little time to figure out what they want to do about us."

Infinity had navigational shields, useful to deflect any space debris away from her hull. She also had much stronger screening that could be used to deflect an attack from an outside and hostile force. Peter chose to leave those screens down as a show of goodwill and trust. And if his gamble proved to be the wrong move, he was pretty certain he could dispatch any incoming fire long enough to get the screens up and his ship far away.

But he had a pretty good idea that the people on the planet below wouldn't start shooting at his ship. Whether or not they would do any talking to his ship however remained to be seen. If their old friend, the fleet commander, had been correct about his people's reaction to what had happened in the past, then they might not want to come face to face with the survivors.

Peter settled into the command chair to wait. Liz had been silently standing nearby the entire time.

"Do you think they'll respond?" she asked.

"I hope so," Peter answered. "It would be a shame to have come all this way for nothing."

"And if they don't?"

"Well," Peter said, blowing out a soft sigh. "I'd rather not just drop in uninvited but we might just have to take a single transport down and see how they greet it. I really want to establish contact and I'd like to find out if our friend ever made it back home."

"So do I," Liz said, placing her hand on Peter's arm.

After an hour of silence from the planet had passed, Peter wondered if they would have to brazen it out and send down an uninvited delegation after all. They had to know, even if the old man's ship had failed to return, who their visitors were.

Should he send a new message, assuring them that there was no ill will toward their people from the people of New Earth? Would they even believe such a message? Were they so ashamed of their role in what had happened that they would refuse to even speak about it or even officially acknowledge it?

All of these thoughts raced through Peter's mind as the minutes silently ticked away. The one advantage of his prolonged life he had discovered, was that without the pressure of time weighing upon them, the human race had become masters of patience. They literally had all of the time in the universe to wait out just about everyone else out there.

"Incoming message," communications called out suddenly. "They are sending visual and audio. Translator is up and syncing translated audio with the visual portion of the transmission."

Peter felt the slight squeeze of Liz's hand and he got up out of the chair, facing the front of the bridge. The front of the bridge appeared to be made of glass, but was instead a transparent wall of solid metal. One of the engineers who had designed the ship had been a Star Trek fan and had dubbed the material "transparent aluminum" even though the substance in front of Peter bore no molecular resemblance to aluminum at all.

"On screen," Peter ordered and the forward view of the approaching planet was replaced by the projected transmission from below.

A group of seven Wolfians, standing behind some type of slate-like slab of gray that served as a table, appeared on the screen. With some slight variations, all seven looked very much like the manager had when he had revealed his true form on Earth. They wore no clothing, nor was there any obvious way to determine what sex they were. Some wore jeweled stones on necklaces, others had bands of silver on their arms and only one had both. It was this one, standing in the center, who addressed the ship.

"Greetings, *Infinity*," the computer translated. "The Council of Elders welcomes you to Siskiri. It pleases us to see that the people of Earth have at last joined the races that travel the great void. It also pleases us to hear that you come in peace and we invite you to send your emissaries to us at your convenience."

"Thank you, sir," Peter replied, fighting to keep the sigh of relief from escaping as he spoke. "We look forward to speaking with you in person and very soon."

"As do we. May I ask your name?"

"I am Peter Childress."

The name sent a shockwave through the seven elders, each quickly glancing at the others. They clearly recognized the name, which told Peter and Liz that the manager had made it home after all.

"Are you the same Childress…" the lead elder's voice trailed off.

"Yes," Peter replied. "I am the one your fleet commander left to rebuild our planet after the accident."

Peter had deliberately chosen the word accident over any other descriptive term, hoping to assure the elders that no ill will remained for them to be concerned about. What impact his words had he could not discern. Wolfian, no they were called Siskirian, he reminded himself firmly, faces were damn near impossible to read.

"Then we have much to discuss indeed, Peter Childress," the lead Elder said finally. "We will send coordinates to you for your landing craft. We await your arrival. Until then."

The transmission ended and the exterior view of Siskiri returned. The bridge remained silent for a few moments.

"Well," Peter said, finally breaking the silence. "That's a promising start at least. For now, I think, it should be just Liz and me going down on the first trip."

Of all of the crew, only Peter and Liz had been born before the accident. Having the people most impacted by what had happened assuring the Siskirians that the two species could move forward in friendship and peace seemed to be an important first step.

"Once we have established contact," he continued. "And if they agree, I'd like for all of us to go planet side before we depart. Let's set the table well for the ships that will follow, make it easier on them, shall we?"

Peter felt a little nervous as he and Liz boarded the two-man transport and flew out of the docking bay. The small black ship slipped into Siskirian atmosphere and headed for the destination that the coordinates would lead them to.

What appeared to be a major city, likely the capital, quickly came into view and a flight of three Siskirian aircrafts linked up with their transport to escort them to a landing pad near the tallest structure in the city. All of the structures were made of a reddish limestone and none reached higher than five or six stories into the cloudless, pale orange sky. The Siskirian ships flew on as the Earth ship settled on the pad.

Even before Peter and Liz could get out, a party of two dozen or so Siskirians stepped out onto the pad, led by the seven Elders. Peter checked to make sure the small translator, a small black box attached to his belt and programmed in Siskiri, was activated and Liz followed suit. Cracking open the hatch, the two stepped out into the dry, arid air. With no breeze, it felt very much like a warm summer day that could be found in any Earth desert.

"Greetings, Peter Childress," the lead Elder said as he stepped forward. "I bid you welcome to Ishe, the capital city of Siskiri. I am Neh'wye, Elder Prime of the Council of Elders. We are pleased to meet your people for the first time."

"As are we, Elder Neh'wye," Peter replied. "This is my wife, Liz. Our peoples have much to discuss and to share with one another."

"Then let us begin," Neh'wye said, extending his arm toward the building entrance. "Come inside where we can begin our talks in comfort."

Neh'wye led the two human visitors inside, both of the visitors having to duck slightly to get past the low overhang, with the rest of the welcoming party following behind. After a few yards along the interior corridor, they stepped into an open area that had been set up as a reception space. All but two of the chairs were of a perfect size for the hosts while a couch of sorts, obviously hastily constructed, had been placed in the room to accommodate the larger visitors.

A table of refreshments, pitchers of a greenish liquid and platters of several types of root vegetables that bore some resemblance to carrots and potatoes of varying colors, had been placed on the surface, nearer to the seats for the Siskirians. A smaller table had been set up next to the couch and held a pitcher of clear water and a dark brown bread.

The difference in fare lent to Peter's belief that the manager had made it back and reported. This was confirmed by Neh'wye's next words.

"Please be seated," he said as he took his own seat. "The water and bread is safe for you to consume. I fear our standard fare would not be agreeable to your metabolisms."

Liz reached over and took a slice of the bread while Peter poured them each some water. The Elders followed suit. The bread looked very much like pumpernickel but tasted closer to sourdough.

"This is very good," she said, creating a stir of pleasure among the Siskiri.

"It is something of a delicacy for us," Neh'wye said. "There is a very small region here on Siskiri where the grain will grow and we have never been able to successfully transplant it to another world. We are delighted that you like it."

A few quiet minutes followed as food and drink were consumed. Peter used the quiet to try to formulate the best way to broach the subject of the manager's fate but Neh'wye opened the door for them.

"We are pleased to see your species take its place among the stars," Neh'wye said, putting down his plate.

"How long have you been traveling beyond your home world?"

"For a few centuries now," Peter said. "At first, we stayed closer to our home sun. But now, we are starting to move further out, to seek out the other civilizations that we know are out here."

"We were not certain you would ever venture out," Neh'wye replied. "Nor that you would ever come here, given the incident that occurred so long ago."

"We have always considered it to be a terrible accident," Liz said. "And nothing more than that. When your fleet commander departed our world, we assured him that we all felt this way."

"But so many of you had perished," Neh'wye said. "We were told that the number of your species alone was in the billions at the time. How could you ever forgive so much loss of life?"

"Billions died, yes," Peter replied. "But we understood there had been no malice involved. It wasn't even a case of negligence or even a mistake by your fleet commander or by one of his crew. It was a fluke, a once in a trillion set of circumstances, and nothing more than that. There was no blame to assign it to other than to fate itself.

That is how we feel about it. And we do not hold him or your people accountable for it."

"So he told our council when he finally returned," Neh'wye said.

"Besides," Liz added. "I think he more than atoned for his role in the accident by what he did afterwards. He literally saved our species and gave us our only chance to survive."

"Yes, he did that," Neh'wye answered. "But his methods…"

"Were the only option he had to ensure our survival," Peter interrupted. "He did not undertake it lightly, but he understood it was his only choice. As you can see, we've done quite well and we hope by establishing contact with your people that you will come to see that as well."

"Indeed," Neh'wye said. "Understanding is the greatest reason for contact between two peoples. It has been some time since we have contacted a new world. Shortly after his return, we stopped sending out exploration parties. We did not want to ever again have such a role in the destruction of that which we had been seeking out."

"That saddens me to hear," Liz said. "There are just too many new wonders to experience out there, even for your world, to stop seeking them out."

"We wanted no more blood to be upon our heads," Neh'wye replied softly. "But perhaps, with your arrival here and bearing us no ill will, we might reconsider and return to the great void again."

"That would please us too, Elder," Peter said, pouncing on the chase to bring up the manager's fate. "As I would expect that it would have pleased the fleet commander. Could you tell us, as it seems apparent that he did make it back, what became of him?"

There was another disquieting pause as the elders exchanged glances.

"After he returned and made his full report to the Council," Neh'wye said. "He was exiled from Siskiri to live alone on one of our outer moons. It was a desolate, frozen moon with just enough of an atmosphere to provide breathable air and water. He was provided with a shelter and supplies to live out his natural life."

"Did none of his family go with him?" Liz asked.

"His family disowned him. He went to his exile alone. A monitor informed us when his life functions had ceased and power was shut down to the shelter."

"So he was never given a burial ceremony?" Peter asked in a hushed tone.

The Siskiri traditions, they knew from the information the manager had left behind, had called for the deceased to be cremated and his or her ashes to be spread in the sky above their home land.

"No, Peter Childress," Neh'wye answered. "No one has ever set foot on that moon since. His body has remained alone, untouched since death came for him. It has likely been preserved by the constant freezing cold of the moon where it lies reposed as it has since the moment of death."

A tear slowly trickled down Liz's cheek, creating something of a stir among the Siskiri as Peter considered his next words.

"Our ship will be here for a few more days," Peter finally began. "Other ships will follow to set up an embassy, if you will allow it, and to exchange more information. But our ship's destination lies much further away. Before we depart your system, we would like to travel out to that moon and pay our respects to him, if that is permitted."

"It is a custom of your people?" Neh'wye asked.

"It is," Liz answered.

"Very well," Neh'wye said. "It seems you have that right, if you wish it. We will provide you the coordinates before your departure."

"Thank you," Liz said.

"Elder?" called out one of the Siskiri who appeared to have been an aide.

"Yes, Kiz'et?"

"I ask permission to lead them out to the moon when the time comes."

"Are you certain of this?" Neh'wye asked, an expression on his face that was close to what a scowl would have been on a human's face.

"Yes, Elder," the younger Siskiri said firmly but respectfully. "Perhaps no other time would be more appropriate than now."

"Very well," Neh'wye said with a sigh. "Perhaps you are correct at that. When the Earth ship departs, you will lead it out to the moon. In the meantime," Neh'wye continued, turning away from the aide. "You must tell us all that has happened since our fleet commander left your world."

The *Infinity* remained in orbit for an Earth week, her crew all spending at least a full day on the planet and by the time their visit had come to an end, they had related the entire history of New Earth while the Siskiri had returned the favor regarding their own history.

As the visit drew to an end, the groundwork for an embassy had been laid. A message had been sent back home to give the all clear for the next ship to visit. This one would stay longer. But the *Infinity* had another galaxy to explore and it was time for her to get underway. But first, there was one last task to complete here in her home galaxy.

Kiz'et flew his little one-man transport up to the *Infinity*, where it fit nicely among the slightly larger human transports in the ship's bay. Peter and Liz gave their guest a quick tour of the Earth ship while the crew prepared to depart Siskiri. Once the tour reached the bridge, Peter gave the order to break orbit and set course for the moon the Siskiri had named, Yr, where the manager's body reposed.

Kiz'et had taken up station nearer the navigation area, but seemed a little out of sorts to the human crew.

"Kiz'et," Liz asked as she stepped closer to him. "Are you all right?"

"I am fine," he replied. "I am merely anxious as to what we will find when we arrive at Yr."

"Why?"

"The individual you knew as the manager," he replied, his voice barely above a whisper yet it managed to carry across the bridge. "He was my ancestor, Fleet Commander Laz'rus."

Liz exchanged a quick glance of surprise with Peter, who joined the conversation.

"But I thought your family had disowned him," Peter said as he got nearby. "Why are you coming out here with us?"

"Because I have long felt our family," Kiz'et replied, "that our entire people, had wronged him. I cannot give him a proper burial, but I can at least stand beside his body and tell his spirit that not all of us have shunned him so."

"I think he would like that very much," Liz said, laying a gentle hand on Kiz'et's cheek.

Peter stood there in silent thought, until the others noticed the faraway look on his face. Taking note that he had suddenly become the center of attention, Peter stepped back to the command chair, but there was a slight smile on his face.

"Perhaps we can do a little better than that," he said aloud as he took his seat. But he would say no more, not even to Liz when they boarded one of the larger transports to head to the surface after the *Infinity* had taken up orbit around Yr.

Kiz'et flew his ship out first, with Peter and Liz following behind in their own, both quickly descending. Within minutes, they landed next to an abandoned structure on a snow-covered sheet of ice. The system's red sun provided some light and the atmosphere was just within breathable norms for both Siskirian and human lifeforms. But it was bitterly cold and all three were clothed in parkas and thick clothing to help fight off the cold.

"What a terrible place to spend the last years of one's life," Liz remarked as they looked around.

"The Council at the time felt it was a suitable punishment," Kiz'et replied, a hint of bitterness in his voice. "There were other moons he could have been sent to that would have been more comfortable, if not as lonely."

"No one spoke up for him?" Peter asked.

"None," Kiz'et replied. "It must have seemed to him that the whole of our species had turned against him. No one from his fleet was alive by the time he returned. There was no one to defend him but himself and he offered no defense."

"Damn him," Peter exclaimed softly, sadly. "I was afraid he would do something like that."

They walked over to the structure and Peter caught himself at the last second. He had been about to knock on the door first. With a wry shake of his head, he grasped the handle and pushed the door open.

As they entered, they found a simple cabin with a small area for preparing food, a table, a desk and a bed. Lying on the bed, as if he had simply gone to sleep, was Laz'rus.

"At least he died at peace," Kiz'et said as he stepped over to the corpse.

Peter looked around and found food and supplies, frozen solid of course, so they could rule out their friend having starved to death. It did appear that he had died of natural causes.

"I always wondered what he was really like," Kiz'et said as he stood over his ancestor. "I wish we could do something for him other than leave him here like this. But his body cannot be taken home nor would the Council approve my taking him elsewhere for a proper burial."

"How long was he out here alone?" Liz asked.

"In your years?" Kiz'et replied with a question. "He was here for one hundred years before he died. He has lain right here ever since with no hope of anyone giving him a proper death ceremony."

"Perhaps it was best that no one did," Peter said quietly as he knelt by Laz'rus. Kiz'et looked at Liz, but she could only shake her head in response. She had no idea what Peter meant either.

"What do you mean?" Kiz'et finally asked.

"There was an ancient people, back on Earth," Peter replied as he kept his gaze on Laz'rus. "They were called the Egyptians and they were so close to discovering immortality. They had one part of the equation figured out, preserving the body. They just never sorted out what to do next."

Peter paused, laying his open right palm on Laz'rus' chest, about where the heart of a Siskirian was located, and then he closed his eyes in concentration.

"You see," he resumed. "What we call the soul, or the spirit, is really just energy. And when the body dies, that energy is imprinted deep within every cell, imprinted on the DNA even and there it lies until the body is repaired and, if you will, re-energized."

Peter stopped talking then. What he had decided to do not even he was certain he had the power to accomplish. But he knew he owed it to this being to try. It had been centuries since Peter had ever employed the ability Laz'rus had given him. He hadn't needed it any longer. But now, he would use it just this one more time.

Kiz'et and Liz both gasped as Laz'rus' corpse began to glow with a soft, shimmering blue light that spread out from Peter's hand and over the length of the body underneath. Then, the body itself seemed to lose its Siskirian form for a few moments, becoming a blur of bluish light. When the glow faded, a human body now lay on the bed and the form was a very familiar one. It was the body of the manager, dressed in the same suit he had worn in the hotel. Peter had altered the DNA to re-create the same body Laz'rus had appeared in back on Earth.

And it was breathing, the chest gently rising and falling.

Then the eyes fluttered open and the man bolted upright, looking wildly about until his gaze settled on the visitors in the room. Then his eyes opened even wider.

"Peter, Liz," he exclaimed, then he took in the Siskirian in the room, registered the rest and realized exactly where they were. "But how?"

"It's a very long story, my friend," Peter replied with a laugh as Liz darted forward to give Laz'rus a hug. "Starting with the fact that it has been over a thousand years since you left Earth and nine centuries have passed since you died here. And we'll be happy to fill you in on all that has happened since we last saw each other and how you came to be resurrected. But there's someone here you should meet. His name is Kiz'et."

"Greetings great-great-grandfather," Kiz'et said, still in shock. "I do not yet understand how this is so, but I am happy to see you, even in this form."

Laz'rus looked down, taking in for the first time his change in body form. Suddenly everything snapped into place and he knew exactly how it had occurred and who was responsible.

"I am happy to meet you, Kiz'et," Laz'rus said. "I assume that I am still exiled, given the present state of my body. You say I died centuries ago?"

"It pains me to say both facts are completely true," Kiz'et said. "I was barely able to get permission to attend with Peter and Liz when they came to pay their respects. We are the first to ever visit this moon since you arrived. I doubt permission would have been given had the Council known of Peter's intentions."

"Better to ask forgiveness," Peter said in a not at all apologetic tone. "Than it is to ask for permission. Wouldn't you agree?"

"Indeed," Laz'rus replied. "So I have been given another lease on life. But since I cannot go home, what kind of life will it be if only my one descendent can visit me?"

"I was wondering," Peter said. "As we're heading off to explore another galaxy, if you might want to come along with us. We could use an experienced explorer. Perhaps, by the time we get back, Kiz'et and his children's children can talk the Council into expunging your record."

"Your voyage will last that long," Laz'rus exclaimed. "But how will I live that…"

His voice trailed off as the answer struck him. Peter had simply done to him what he had done to Peter and the survivors back on Earth a millennium ago.

"How long will I live?"

"Who knows," Peter replied with a smile. "Maybe for thousands of years, maybe forever. No one on Earth has died of old age yet, hell none of us are even showing the slightest effect of aging."

"An eternity to explore and to discover," Laz'rus said to himself, the shock of his resurrection fading into the joy of a new chance at life. "How could I say no."

"Then welcome aboard," Peter said. "Kiz'et, you're welcome to come along if you like. But it will be a very long time before we return. You might not live to see your home world again."

"Thank you for your offer, Peter," Kiz'et said after a long pause. "But I would miss my world too much. Besides, I will be of better service to my ancestor if I go back and convince the Council of the errors of their ways.

"I am happy to have met you, Grandfather," Kiz'et said, holding up a forepaw in the Siskirian sign of farewell. "Even if our meeting was brief. It pleases me to know that you have resumed your rightful place among the great void. I will tell my children and their children of your journeys and that they should look for the day of your return, so that you will be welcomed properly this time. Farewell."

Laz'rus returned the sign and the pair embraced. Kiz'et stepped away, bade farewell to Liz and Peter and returned to his ship to head back to Siskiri. They watched him lift off and the glow of his engine faded into the black sky.

"Is there anything you want to take with you?" Peter asked after the little ship was out of sight.

"Nothing at all," Laz'rus replied. "There's nothing here for me."

"Then let's get going," Peter said.

"You're really going to another galaxy?"

"Yes," Liz said. "You're going to be amazed by our ship and how far we have traveled."

"I can just imagine," Laz'rus said as they boarded the transport.

"You know," Peter said minutes later as he flew the transport back up to the ship. "There is one thing we're going to need to do for you before you officially join the crew."

"What is that?"

"Well, your Siskirian name is damn near unpronounceable in normal human speaking and you are definitely now a human being. We're going to have to give you a new name."

"I assume you have something in mind for me," Laz'rus replied as Liz, having figured out where Peter was heading, laughed lightly.

"Oh, most certainly," Peter said with a warm smile as the transport settled down on the deck of the *Infinity's* bay. "It really is the only possible choice, you know. Welcome aboard the *Infinity*, Lazarus."

EPILOGUE

For centuries, the Thoac had searched the skies, seeking other life. They knew, after eons of looking into their night skies—when their four moons weren't shining so brightly, stargazing was possible—that they lived at the very edge of their galaxy. They also knew that many other galaxies existed in the universe; they could even just make out some details about their closest neighbor.

It was a smaller galaxy than theirs, similarly shaped but with a slight difference in appearance in the outer edges. It also seemed to head right for their galaxy, but the impact was not expected to occur for a very great amount of time.

They had even begun venturing out into the void, to seek out others, to know that they weren't all alone in the vastness that lay beyond their atmosphere. But so far, they had yet to make contact with another intelligent species.

The name for their home world was Voesa, they called their galaxy, Lierith. Their neighbor galaxy, Ibiran.

And they despaired of ever meeting any life from their own galaxy, much less their approaching neighbor.

Laralla was the head of exploration for the Thoac. She had devoted her life to the pursuit of knowledge of the universe, how it had come to be and the Thoac's place within it. Like those that had come before her, she had all but given up hope that she would live long enough to see her people make first contact. They simply did not have the capability yet to travel to the closest star where they believed other life might exist.

She never dreamed that all she would need to do to make first contact was to be in orbit around the sixth planet of her own solar system.

A massive black ship, a giant wing in shape with pod-like areas that were lit up like the fire bugs of her home world's swamps, and strange markings in gold simply appeared before her. It seemed as if a bubble had formed and the ship sailed from its center and into her view.

Her fingers flew across her control panel, scanning the alien ship in front of her, activating the translator program even as she searched for any signal from the ship for it to translate into her tongue. She quickly sent off a message to Voesa, the fourth planet in the system, so they would know what had happened to her out here, in case the alien was hostile.

After a few moments, an opening appeared on the side of the vessel facing her own ship. She could see a well-lit landing area, big enough to easily fit her ship within. But nothing flew out from that bay and she suddenly realized that this was an invitation for her to come aboard.

But was it safe? Did she dare go inside?

Suddenly, she shook herself. *Silly girl*, she thought as she tapped the controls to send her ship toward the opening, *if they wanted me dead, they could no doubt have already done so. And this was why she was out here in the first place. To find new life and here it had found her.*

Her ship settled gently onto the deck, the door closing behind her. Her ship reported the atmosphere in the bay was well within tolerable limits. She could walk out there without a suit. She popped open the hatch and stepped outside, marveling at the construction of the ship she had entered.

Off against the far wall, a door slid open and three of the strangest figures she had even seen entered the bay and walked toward her, *on two legs!* She moved a little closer to her ship, her eight legs poised to leap back into her ship, the small hairs on her body standing so straight that they brushed the floor beneath her.

The creatures had two more legs higher up on their bodies, with strange looking appendages attached to the ends. Their heads, if you could call them that, were of a kind that she had never seen anywhere in all of her travels. And they only had two eyes. How could anything see properly without eight eyes?

They were strange. They were bizarre. They were… *alien.*

"Greetings," said one as it towered over her, even though it remained several feet away, and her eyes went wide as she realized that she could understand their words. Either they knew her language, unlikely as the sounds did not match the movements of whatever orifice that was on their heads where the sound seemed to come from, or they had a very sophisticated and advanced translator.

"My name is Lazarus," it continued. "And this is Peter and Liz Childress. We are very happy to meet you. We have come a very, very long way to get here. Welcome aboard the *Infinity.*"

ABOUT THE AUTHOR

Richard Paolinelli is an author and award-winning sportswriter and editor. His first fiction credit, working on the 1986 graphic novel series, *Seadragon*, preceded a 25-year newspaper career. After retiring, Richard has returned to fiction writing with the four-book Jack Del Rio series, two novelettes, *Legacy of Death* and *The Invited*, as well as a science fiction novel, *Maelstrom*. He has also written two historical sports non-fiction books – *From The Fields* and *Perfection's Arbiter*. When not writing, he and his wife are usually spoiling their grandchildren.

51705663R00185

Made in the USA
San Bernardino, CA
30 July 2017